SNOWMEN AND SORCERY

A Spellbinder Bay Cozy Paranormal Mystery - Book Four

SAM SHORT

www.samshortauthor.com

Created with Vellum

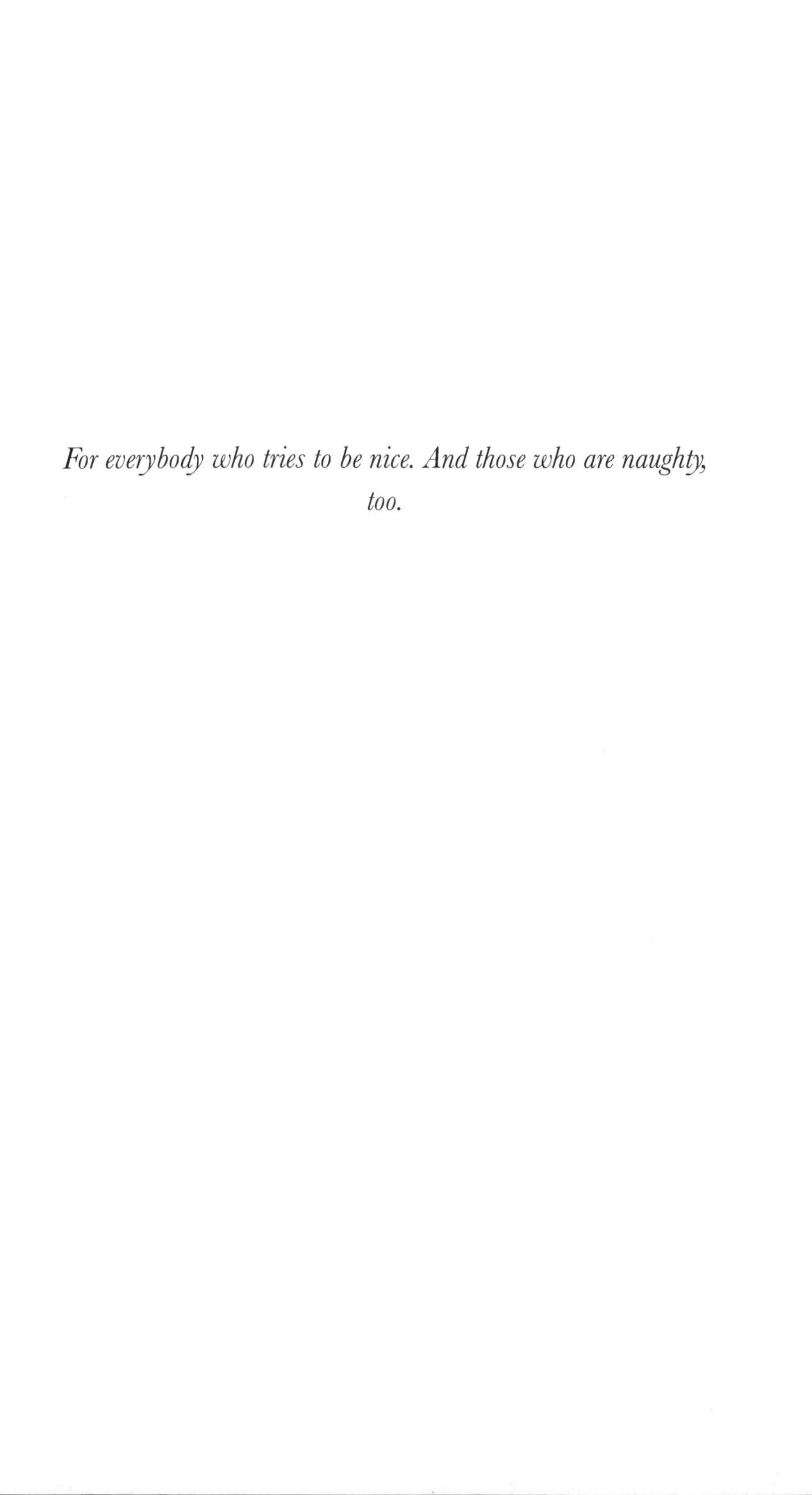

For everybody who tries to be nice. And those who are naughty, too.

Chapter 1

"I don't want to die two days before Christmas!" screeched Reuben. "I've got plans!"

Time slowed for Millie Thorn. As she gripped the door handle, she watched the man sitting alongside her as he attempted to control the car.

His face illuminated by the instrument panel, he cursed under his breath as he battled with the steering wheel.

He jerked it to the left, but the car's path remained true, travelling into the tunnel of light afforded by the headlights. The tunnel of light which led through the driving snowstorm, to the apex of the tight bend, beyond which lurked the sheer drop from the craggy Scottish mountain.

The drop which road signs had been warning of for the last three miles.

Hindsight was a fabulous concept. If she survived the next few moments, Millie would speak of the incident by explaining, *with hindsight, we probably shouldn't have decided to navigate that road during a blizzard. In fact, we should never have gone to Scotland. We knew the weather was going to be bad, but we risked the journey anyway.*

Judith screamed, and Millie turned to look into the large back seat of the SUV. The normally unflustered blue of Judith's eyes had taken on a desperate new hue. Fuelled by the adrenalin that no doubt coursed through her body, her eyes gleamed in the gloom — electric blue and staring, her pupils large.

She screamed again and clutched her father's shoulder as he battled the steering wheel. "Dad!" she said. "Do something!"

The driver grunted, his eyes wide as the car slithered through deep snow, transporting its occupants nearer and nearer disaster. "I'm trying, darling," he said, his knee jerking as he pumped the brakes. "There's no grip."

Millie estimated that the car would leave the road in about five seconds.

She used the first of those seconds to place her hand on the driver's forearm. "Keep calm, Dad," she said.

The next second came too quickly for her liking, and she used it to ponder irony.

How ironic it would be that after discovering the man sitting next to her was her father, they'd die together two days before Christmas Day, and the day before the birthday that she'd been looking forward to so much. Her first birthday with a father.

The third second allowed her more self-indulgent pondering. She stared ahead, into the night, the driving snow making visibility mercifully less clear. She pondered her good luck. Not only had she discovered she had a father, but she'd gained a sister, too.

Sergeant David Spencer had adopted Judith when she'd been a toddler struggling with life as an orphaned witch. At that time in his life, the young policeman had been ignorant of the paranormal world, but having shown such kindness to the young witch, the paranormal community was not ignorant of him.

Taking him as one of their own, Sergeant Spencer had lived among the community of Spellbinder Bay for the last three decades. A great man, he'd brought Judith up to be the sort of person that Millie was proud to call a sibling.

Three and a half seconds had passed, and Millie revisited irony as the car left the smooth ice rink surface of the road and thumped and bumped across the rough ground leading to the drop.

How ironic that having found this beautiful family, she would plummet with them to the depths of a valley, deep in the Scottish Highlands.

The fourth second arrived, and Millie used it to look into the coal-black eye of the cockatiel which sat on her lap. Her familiar. Her companion.

Yes, Reuben was rude, short-tempered, greedy and insolent, but she loved him.

The bird stared back at her. "If I die, I'm blaming

you!" he squawked, the red patches on his cheeks bright, even in the gloom. "You'd better do something! Right now!"

What could she do? Her powers didn't extend as far as miracles. How could she possibly prevent a heavy vehicle from careering over a cliff edge?

Her magical repertoire had improved immensely in the last year but was frustratingly void of a spell powerful enough to prevent the looming catastrophe.

As Reuben screeched at her, demanding she do something, Millie stopped breathing. She ignored the thumping of her heart against her ribs. *Maybe she could do something.*

She delved deep within herself, tugging at the strands of energy she imagined controlled the magic in her chest. She pulled at them, one by one, her imagination a puppet master and his marionette attempting a new routine.

Then, as clear as the sound of Judith's scream as the vehicle's front wheels dropped into nothingness, Edna Brockett's face appeared in her mind's eye — the witch who'd once almost scared Millie to death, and the owner of the log cabin they'd been travelling towards when the rubber holding their car on the road had given up on them.

When Edna had found out that Millie had a new family, she'd insisted that the father and daughters used the cabin she owned to spend a magical Christmas in together. It had been standing empty for far too long, she'd explained. It needed some life inside it.

They'd taken her up on the offer, each of them excited about living as a regular human being for a while, away from a paranormal town. Even if it was just for a few days.

But now, as the car plummeted, the image of Edna still vivid, Millie remembered something the witch had once said to her. She'd told Millie that to fully control her magic, she only needed to think hard enough about what she wanted to happen. It was that simple, the witch had said.

It had never seemed simple to Millie. She was sure that Edna had been an accomplished witch for so long that she'd forgotten the more complicated intricacies of magic. Just thinking hard enough had made simple spells work for Millie, but not the difficult ones. The sort that she needed right now.

Her father gripped her wrist, rubbing his thumb along her flesh, and her sister's screams filled the compact space. *Both preparing for the inevitable.*

Tugging at one last string, drawing her magic into the open, Millie thought hard about what she wanted to happen, her eyes squeezed tightly closed.

Her fingers tingling as energy flowed through them, she concentrated intensely. She told her magic what she wanted it to do — sending urgent instructions to the energy at her fingertips, hoping it would obey.

She gritted her teeth. It wasn't going to work. It

was too late. The car would slam into the rocky mountainside soon. She'd failed. She was too weak a witch to save her family.

Then, she noticed the silence. Judith no longer screamed, and her father's gasping breaths were calmer.

Judith spoke, her voice gentle. "Millie, keep doing whatever it is you're doing, but I really think you should open your eyes."

Chapter 2

Her hands fizzing with magic, Millie dared to open her eyes. She blinked. Then she stared through the windscreen at the view before her.

Instead of jagged rocks, awaiting them at the base of the valley, she saw star-speckled skies. She blinked again, remembering what Judith had advised — she must keep the spell alive.

Locking onto the thought that controlled her magic, she broadcast it once more — the simple command consisting of just three short words. *Fly, car. Fly!*

As if to confirm what Millie was seeing, her father squeezed her arm. "You're making the car fly."

Staring at her father, Millie broke into a grin, magic bubbling in her chest. "I'm making a car fly!"

Judith gave a whoop of joy and leaned through

the gap between the car's front two seats. "You're flying! We're flying!"

Cocking his head, Reuben fluttered from Millie's lap to the dashboard, where he stood peering through the glass at the canvas of stars beyond. "Are we nearly there yet? We've been travelling for eight hours!"

"Is that all you have to say to her?" said Judith. "She just saved our lives."

"You should be thanking me," said Reuben. "I told her to. I implicitly recall saying, '*you'd better do something. Right now*.' Then she made the car fly. It was my doing."

"Can we pause for a moment and reflect on what just happened," said the sisters' father. "We could have died down there."

"If we must, Sergeant Spencer," said Reuben.

"We must," said the policeman. He smiled at Millie. "You saved our lives, thank you. How did you do it? How *are* you doing it?"

Staring at her hands, Millie shrugged. "I sent a thought through my magic. I asked the car to fly, and it flew. It's still flying."

"Hovering, actually," said Reuben. "There's a difference."

A blast of cold air whipped through the car as Judith opened her window. "Did you ask it to glow neon red, too?"

"Not that I remember," smiled Millie. "The car has red paintwork. The magic is making it brighter, that's all."

Suddenly, the car lurched to the side, and Judith squealed. "What was that?" she said, her fingers on Millie's shoulder, her nails digging deep.

"It's okay," Millie assured her. "I thought about making the car move, and it responded, but if you don't remove your nails from my shoulder, I might lose control of the spell completely. They're quite sharp, you know?"

"Sorry," said Judith, brushing blonde strands of hair from her face. "It frightened me. Do you think you should take us down now? We're at least a hundred feet above the road. It's a little unnerving."

"Actually," said Millie, adding more energy to the spell which kept them in the air. "I'm considering flying us to Kilgrettin."

"Do you think you could do that?" asked Sergeant Spencer.

"I think so," said Millie, confidence growing within her as she explored the spell connecting her to the SUV. "I really think I can do it."

"*Think*?" said Judith. "Don't you *think* you should just put the car back on the road. Maybe it would be safer?"

"Safer?" said Sergeant Spencer. "Those roads down there are not safe. We shouldn't have risked coming. We might not even get through to Kilgrettin. It's still twenty miles away, and you saw how deep the snow was getting. The snow's died down for now, but more clouds are moving in. We'd be silly to try and drive the rest of the way."

"We could drive back the way we came," suggested Judith.

"The last town we passed is over thirty miles away," said her father. "We might not make it. And if we got stuck, there's no mobile signal. We couldn't phone for help. This is a desolate part of The Highlands. I say we let Millie try."

"I knew I shouldn't have come with you people," grumbled Reuben. "I hate cars. I should have flown. I might not be a crow, but I can still fly in a straight line. I'd have been there by now!"

Sergeant Spencer sighed. "I can open the sunroof if you'd like? The dashboard thermometer says it's freezing out there. Still, I'm certain adverse weather conditions are nothing a hardy little bird such as yourself can't handle." He gave a deep-throated chuckle. "What do you say? Shall I open the sunroof so you can launch yourself from this lovely warm car and navigate a route over the mountains through the cold wind and snow?

"It's the twenty-third of December today, Reuben. I doubt you'd find your way to the log cabin before the first of January, let alone in time for Millie's birthday tomorrow or Christmas Day."

The bird stiffened. "I could easily find my way through the storm if I wanted to," he said defiantly. "But I feel I'd be letting Millie down. As her familiar, it's my job to be here to offer her advice and support, should she require it. I'd be letting both her and myself down if I were to abandon her. Reluctantly, I shall continue the journey by car. Preferably by flying car."

Giggling, Millie reached for the bird and tickled him on the cheek, the car rocking as she moved. "I appreciate your loyalty. I'm pleased that you want to stay here with me."

"Although we all know you wanted to stay behind in Spellbinder Bay instead of accompanying your witch on her trip to Scotland," said Judith, a smile hovering on her lips. "And we all know you're far too lazy to even consider flying the rest of the way."

"There's a pantry stocked full of food back in Windy-dune Cottage, and there's a fantastic TV schedule lined up for Christmas, so yes, I did want to stay at home! As for laziness — you're a fine one to talk," scoffed Reuben. "You were too lazy to pack your own suitcase before we left. My witch had to do it for you!"

"She offered," said Judith. "I'm not the best at knowing what to pack. I wouldn't have known where to start! At least I didn't try and sneak a half-eaten jam doughnut and a tub of ice-cream with a broken lid into Millie's suitcase!"

"I was thinking ahead," retorted Reuben. "I doubt those savages in Scotland have heard of ice-cream! I must have my ice-cream! It's a staple food in my diet!"

"Only because your health is protected by magic, Reuben," said Millie. "Imagine you were a normal cockatiel. You'd be living off seeds and fruit."

The little bird shuddered. "I can't imagine how

those poor creatures get through life," he said in a subdued voice. He fixed an eye on Judith. "I need my ice-cream. It keeps me sane! That's why I sneaked it into the suitcase. Do you have any idea of the sort of strength and agility a cockatiel must possess to achieve such a feat? It wasn't easy. And then you thought you would just take it out and put it back in the freezer! You disgust me, Judith. You really do!"

"Firstly, the ice-cream would have melted by the time we got an hour out of Spellbinder Bay," said Judith. "We've been on the road all day. It would have been liquid by now and would've ruined Millie's clothes. And secondly, but most importantly, considering our current location… the Scottish people are not savages, Reuben. You must believe us when we tell you that Braveheart is not based on modern-day Scotland. It's a film. It's make-believe loosely based on history. There will be plenty of ice-cream where we're going, and the people will be lovely."

"There had better be, and *they'd* better be," answered Reuben. "And washing machines? Will they have washing machines in Scotland?"

Millie frowned. "Why do you ask?"

"I was simply recalling something Judith once said about melting ice-cream and ruined clothes," said the cockatiel through a yawn. "It's not important."

Sergeant Spencer cleared his throat. "I think our life in a paranormal community has desensitised us against extraordinary events. May I remind the three of you that we are currently seated in a vehicle which is hanging in the air above the unforgiving mountains of Scotland. I really think we should be concentrating on that fact, rather than who packed what, in which suitcase."

"You're right," answered Millie. She ran her eyes over the landscape spanning before them. Snow-capped mountains soared above them, tinted silver by the moon, and a gaping valley led the eye into the dark distance. "I'm flying us to Kilgrettin! Should I follow the route the road takes?"

"The road is barely visible. It's covered in snow," said Sergeant Spencer, glancing below them, his hand tightening on the steering wheel as he did so. He gulped. "We are quite high. Are you sure you can keep this spell going? Making a car fly is a big ask, even for an accomplished witch. Do you really think *you* can do it?" His face dropped as he realised what he'd said, and he spoke his next sentence urgently. "That doesn't mean that I don't think you're an accomplished witch! You know what I meant — I meant an older witch, like Edna. One with more experience than you have!"

Millie smiled as she ignored him. Then she took a deep breath and concentrated. Picturing the car as a steam train chugging sluggishly away from a station, she allowed herself a smile as the car began moving.

Jerking a little as she guided it forward, the car gained speed, and Reuben pecked at the windscreen, squawking with delight. "We're moving! We'll get to Kilgrettin in time for dinner! I'm starving!"

Moving slowly and smoothly, the vehicle made a soft humming sound as it gathered speed, pushing through the night sky. Commanding the car to bank left, Millie lined the bonnet up with the peak of a distant mountain and urged the vehicle forward.

"This is amazing! Can you make it go faster?" asked Sergeant Spencer, childlike wonder in his eyes, and his hands still gripping the steering wheel, as if letting go would cause the vehicle to plummet from the sky.

Could she make it go faster? She thought so. Wiping the image of a slow train from her mind, she replaced it with the image of an arrow shot from a bow, sliding frictionless through the air. Thrusting Millie into her seat and throwing Reuben from the dashboard into her lap, the car responded with a burst of alarming acceleration.

Rather than cry out in fear as the SUV gathered speed, darting across the snowscape like a fighter jet, Sergeant Spencer made a loud whooping sound of joy that made Millie laugh. "Oh yeah!" he cried out. "Oh yeah!"

Struggling to escape the g-force pinning him to Millie's stomach, Reuben screeched with frustration. "I'm stuck! Hold me up so I can see!"

Grasping her familiar gently, Millie lifted him to a higher vantage point, and turned to check on her sister. "Are you okay back there?"

Wearing the same expression Millie had seen on her face when they'd ridden a rollercoaster together, Judith gave a series of nods, her pupils large and shining. "Yes!" she managed. "Yes!"

Knowing now that she had as much control over the car as she had over one of her own limbs, Millie gave the vehicle a silent command. *Climb*, she ordered, *climb!*

Imagining the car was a rocket leaving the launch pad at Cape Canaveral, Millie's stomach flipped as the car tilted aggressively. With the view through the windscreen now exclusively of the star filled sky, the car surged upwards.

Screeching, Reuben tumbled from Millie's hand as the car took a vertical route into the night sky. As gravity guided him towards the rear seat of the vehicle, he grabbed Millie's hair with a clawed foot, breaking his fall.

"Ouch!" said Millie, her scalp stinging.

Suddenly, the car tilted, and with a stomach-churning change of direction, hurtled towards the valley far below them.

"Millie!" yelled Sergeant Spencer, one hand on the steering wheel and the other on his youngest daughter's arm, pinching her flesh. "We're falling!"

As Reuben twisted his foot further into her hair, she focussed on her magic, ignoring the pains in her scalp and forearm. The car responded violently, turning on its axis and aiming for the stars again.

Prising her father's strong fingers from her arm,

she removed Reuben from her hair, his foot bringing with it long strands of chestnut. She placed him in the cup holder and sucked in a long breath. "Sorry about that, lady, gentleman and bird," she said as if making a pilot's announcement. "The car travelled through a little turbulence. Although it was Reuben's claws in my scalp which made me lose focus."

"Not funny," said Sergeant Spencer, his knuckles white on the steering wheel. "Do you have full control now?"

Millie nodded, feeling her energy vibrating through the car around her. "I do."

"Then stop flying towards the moon," said her father. "Kilgrettin is north of here. Straighten the car and take us there."

"There's just one thing I want to do first," said Millie, urging the car heavenward.

Watching the ground becoming distant through the side window, Millie waited until the snow-capped mountains resembled little egg-white peaks on a meringue. Then she brought the vehicle back into a forward trajectory and slowed it gently until it hung in the sky, suspended high above the Scottish Highlands.

"Wow," said a voice from the back seat.

"Yes, Judith," said Sergeant Spencer. "Wow."

Millie looked at her father. His face was free of the panic he'd displayed less than thirty seconds before, replaced by peaceful awe that made the hairs on her forearms bristle. "Nice view, isn't it?" she said.

Her father nodded slowly, gazing through the windscreen at the vista that sprawled before them. "Yes," he said, taking his hands from the steering wheel. "It's the most beautiful view I've ever seen."

"It's amazing," said Judith. "I could stay up here forever."

"I must admit," said Reuben, scrambling onto the dashboard. "Scotland looks quite nice from up here. That's not an endorsement of the place, I must add. I'm reserving that judgement until I've had boots on the ground, so to speak."

Then the four of them fell silent, only the sounds of relaxed breathing filling the vehicle as they each enjoyed the view in their own subjective way.

Taking in the vast snowscape, which twinkled beneath the stars and moon, Millie took in every detail of the ground and the sky. Rivers reflected the moonlight as they meandered through mountains and forests, and several small towns and villages sat beneath golden domes of light pollution, while on the distant horizon, a much larger city lit the sky.

Appearing many light-years closer than they were, Millie imagined she could reach out and pluck a star from the sky. She gazed fascinated at the intricate silver threads of detail on the moon's surface, its craters large and imposing.

After a few minutes, she gave the car a silent command, and it began sliding forward, losing altitude as she guided it northward. She pointed at a lone bubble of light cradled in a valley. "That must be Kilgrettin."

"That was something very special," said Sergeant Spencer, as the car lost height.

"And now we know we never have to drive anywhere again," laughed Judith. "Millie can fly us to where we need to be!"

"This is a one-off," said Sergeant Spencer. "You have to promise me that you two girls won't do anything like this again. You'll end up in big trouble if you start joyriding in flying cars."

"I won't do it again," promised Millie. "This was an emergency, but I couldn't resist taking that little detour."

"It was worth it," said her father. "That was an experience I won't forget. But you know the rules, don't you?" He turned to Judith. "You both know the rules."

"No magic is to be used in an area where there is no concealment spell to hide it from the non-paranormal community," stated Millie. She pressed her nose against the car window and stared into space. "I don't see a non-paranormal community out there, Dad, do you?"

"I'm just saying Henry wouldn't be happy if he finds out," said her father. "I don't want either of you using any more magic when this car lands, okay?"

"Henry Pinkerton isn't here, Dad," said Judith. "And he won't be in Kilgrettin. He's enjoying Christmas in Spellbinder Hall."

"But he can sense when somebody uses magic," answered her father. "He'll know."

"No, Dad," said Millie. "It's not like that. He can sense when a new witch uses their magic for the first time, then he goes out into the world to find him or her and offer them a life in our community… like he did with me, but he doesn't tune into every magic spell that's cast. That would drive him mad."

"Especially spells cast by Millie or me," said Judith. "He trusts us, and if he did sense that we'd used magic, he'd assume it was for a good reason." She paused and pointed at the rugged landscape below. "And preventing us from crashing to the bottom of that valley is an excellent reason."

"I'm only asking that you be careful, girls," said Sergeant Spencer, gazing at the stars. "I love you both. I don't want you getting in trouble."

"We'll be careful," promised Millie, guiding the car nearer to the amber glow of the small town at the foot of a mountain.

Slowing the car as they neared Kilgrettin, colourful Christmas lights visible below, Millie opened the glove compartment and retrieved the hand-drawn directions Edna had given them.

She glanced at the map and then at the ground, matching the two until she found the spot in a forest on the far side of the town where she guessed the log cabin was.

"The cabin's over there," she said, pointing. "And look, the roads in the town have been ploughed.

Should I bring us down in town, or head straight for the cabin?"

"Take us to the cabin," said Sergeant Spencer. "The car's glowing like a beacon in the sky. We can't risk being seen. Let's hope nobody has already spotted us. Keep us high and skirt the edges of the town."

Chapter 3

Doing as her father suggested, Millie asked the car to gain altitude, the vehicle reacting immediately. When enough height had been achieved, she flew the car quickly towards the soaring mountains at the westerly edge of town. Following the rugged landmarks, she skirted the town and headed for the spot she'd picked out on the mountainside.

"Bring us lower," said Sergeant Spencer, staring at the ground. "I can't see the cabin yet."

Allowing the car to drop quickly from the sky, Millie scanned the thick forest, looking for clearings in the dense canopy of pine trees.

Then she saw it — moonlight reflecting off the windows giving it away. "There," she said. "That must be it!"

Her father studied it for a moment, and then looked at the map. "Yes," he nodded. "That's it. Look, there's the lane leading to it — it hasn't been ploughed. It's a good job we flew here."

"Then take us down!" demanded Reuben. "Some of us want to start enjoying ourselves."

As the SUV neared ground level, a new problem revealed itself. "It's completely snowed in. There's nowhere to park the car," said Millie.

Inviting a cold blast of wind into the vehicle, which made Reuben squawk with shock, Judith lowered her window and peered at the deep snow below. "Take us a little bit lower, and I'll clear us a parking space in no time," she said, a glint in her eyes.

Millie returned her smile. "Make sure you clear enough snow. You know parking's not my forte," she said through a laugh, as the car dropped from the sky.

When the wheels of the vehicle were close to the snow, Judith cast her spell. Cascades of pretty sparks fell from her fingertips, gliding gracefully towards the ground. The snow sizzled and spat as the sparks landed on it, and soon a river of meltwater was clearing a path through the drifts.

When a patch of ground large enough for two lorries, let alone a medium-sized family SUV had been cleared, the sparks ceased to flow from Judith's fingertips, and she gave her sister a proud smile. "There, you do the flying, I'll do the snow melting. It might not be as glamorous, but it's mine!"

"You've both done wonderfully well today," said Sergeant Spencer, as the car landed with a gentle thump. "I'm proud of you both."

Smiling inwardly, Millie opened the door and stepped into the cold air. Before she'd considered looking at the cabin which would be home for the next few days, her eyes were drawn to the sweeping moonlit view which opened up across the Kilgrettin valley.

Soaring mountains and forested hills led the eye into the distance, and the town of Kilgrettin lay below them like a beautiful model village. Smoke curled lazily from chimneys, and although Millie guessed Kilgrettin was a mile away, she could make out the town's Christmas tree — a tall triangle of colourful light.

"It's beautiful here," said Judith, joining her sister.

"Yes," said Millie. "It is."

"Why don't you two girls have a look around the cabin while I start bringing the luggage in?" suggested their father, tossing the cabin key towards his daughters.

Judith snatched the key from the air, and with a teasing smile, hurried towards the timber door at the top of three snow-topped wooden steps. "I'm going to get the best bedroom!" she laughed.

Judith had opened the door by the time Millie reached her, and the two sisters pushed through the doorway into the dark cabin interior.

Remembering the instructions Edna had given her, Millie used the slivers of moonlight which broke through the snow dusted windows to locate the cupboard containing the fuse box.

Feeling for the master switch, she flicked it upward and looked over her shoulder. "Find a light switch," she said.

Locating a switch near the door, Judith turned on a series of wall-mounted lights, which flickered into life, bathing the cabin's beautiful interior in a soft, warm glow.

Immediately forgetting about claiming the best bedroom, the girls took in their surroundings, both smiling as they studied the open-plan interior.

With a classic kitchen taking up the floor space in one corner, the cabin oozed traditional Scottish character. From the tartan cushions placed neatly on the leather couches, to the oil painting of a bellowing stag hanging over the stone fireplace, the cabin exceeded Millie's expectations. Edna Brockett certainly had better taste than Millie had credited her with.

Smelling overwhelmingly of the aromatic wood the building was constructed from, the cabin offered a myriad of pleasant underlying smells, too.

The heavy scent of leather furniture mingled with the cold freshness of mountain air, and the slightly acrid scent of the soot-blackened hearth brought cosy images of a crackling log fire to mind.

As Sergeant Spencer appeared in the doorway, a suitcase in each hand, a delighted expression spread across his face. He dropped the luggage and gazed around. "This is better than I expected."

Hurrying towards the door near the fireplace,

Judith looked back over her shoulder. "I'm still going to get the best bedroom," she teased.

WITH THE THREE BEDROOMS ALLOCATED, EACH AS desirable as the others, Millie turned on the television for Reuben, who perched happily on the oak coffee table, staring at the vast expanse of screen. "That," he said, admiration in his voice, "is the biggest TV I have ever seen. I'm certainly going to enjoy my stay here, that's for sure."

"There's just one thing missing," said Sergeant Spencer over the sound of the TV. "Christmas decorations. Edna told me there are boxes of them in one of the outhouses. Shall we do it tonight? Or shall we wait until tomorrow?"

"It's Millie's birthday tomorrow!" said Judith. "She doesn't want to spend the day putting up Christmas decorations!"

"It's a stupid day for a birthday if you ask me," said Reuben, his eyes not moving from the cartoon on the screen. "Who has a birthday on Christmas Eve?"

"I didn't really choose it, Reuben," said Millie. "But I don't mind putting up Christmas decorations on my birthday."

Then, with a peculiar sparkle in her eyes, Judith moved closer to a window and peered outside. "We need something to show it's Christmas, and I've got an idea! Follow me!"

Crunching through knee-deep snow, with her father and sister in tow, Judith headed for a tall pine tree, its branches supporting inches of snowfall. She stood next to it, smiling. "What do you think of this for a Christmas tree?" she asked, gazing up at the mature pine.

"We'll cut a smaller tree down tomorrow, Judith," said Sergeant Spencer. "This tree's three times as tall as the cabin! It's far too big to fit inside."

"That's not what I had in mind," teased Judith. Suddenly, sparks erupted from her fingertips, and she coaxed them towards the tip of the tree. When they reached the top, she let them fall.

Sizzling when they met snow, the sparks tumbled like delicate confetti, melting the majority of snow but leaving a dusting on the branches as fine as icing sugar on a cake.

Then Judith lifted her other hand and sent out a fresh surge of bright energy. Beginning as sparks, the energy mutated into glowing tendrils, which twisted and wended their way through the branches of the tree, leaving behind them twinkling Christmas tree decorations as they moved.

When her sister's plan became apparent, Millie stepped closer to the tree, enjoying the pine needle perfume in the air. She drew on her own magic, flinging energy from her fingertips towards the tree. Following her sister's example, she willed her magic to take the form of Christmas decorations and sparkling lights.

In less than a minute the tree was transformed into a Christmas tree adorned with decorations more beautiful than Millie had ever seen.

Golden balls engraved with intricate patterns hung alongside icicle shaped lights, which twinkled in blues and golds, their shimmering reflections mirrored in the snow below the tree.

Delicate strands of energy combined to form garlands of magical tinsel which wrapped around branches and portions of the trunk, making the whole tree glow. Even the pine needles themselves danced with kaleidoscopes of festive colours. One moment gold, and the next red or deep green. Glass baubles sparkled on branches, hanging from golden and silver threads of energy.

"What are you doing?" said Sergeant Spencer, unable to hide the excited sparkle in his eyes. Attempting to appear stern, he furrowed his brow. "You can't do this! We've already spoken about this — you two shouldn't be using any magic. The magic that was used today was because of an emergency. This is not an emergency."

Millie reached for her father's hand. She smiled up at him as he squeezed her fingers. "This is our first Christmas together," she said. "Let's enjoy it." She looked up at the tree, marveling as a glass bauble took on the appearance of the moon. "Look at it. It's beautiful."

Nodding slowly, Sergeant Spencer smiled. "It is beautiful," he agreed. "And I'll let us keep it on two conditions. The first condition is that you magic some sort of fake electrical cable running from the tree to the cabin, so if anybody does happen to visit us here, it's going to look as normal as it can look."

"Consider it done," said Judith, guiding a burst of bright red sparks towards the ground at the base of the tree, where some of the roots were visible.

As the sparks enveloped one of the smaller roots, the gnarly wood's surface became smooth and the root shrank in diameter until it resembled an electricity cable.

Pulling itself from the ground and extending in length, it searched the air like a snake sniffing for prey, and then slithered through the snow towards the cabin. When it got to the building, it pushed itself tight against the wooden wall and lay still. "There," said Judith, pleased with herself. "Now it looks like a normal Christmas tree, but with extremely luxurious decorations."

"What was the second condition?" asked Millie.

Pointing to the very tip of the tree, Sergeant Spencer put an arm around each of the girls. "I've always had a star on the top of my Christmas tree, I don't want this Christmas tree to be any different. Put a star up there, and you can keep the tree."

The sisters exchanged glances and smiled. Lifting their hands in unison, they each sent out a stream of magical energy, both aiming for the tip of the tree. When the two beams of energy reached the top of the pine, they grazed one another, and knowing that her sister would be doing the same, Millie imagined the most beautiful star she could think of. Then, with a flash of light which briefly illuminated the whole of the forest clearing, a star was formed.

Just as Millie was about to step back and admire their work, her magic grazed Judith's beam of energy once more, and without a guiding thought attached to the particles of energy, they reacted in a way she'd not anticipated.

A loud crack echoed through the forest, causing snow to fall from nearby trees. Then, in another blinding flash of light, a ball of magic formed above the tree. It hovered for a second or two, emitting a soft hum before another crack reverberated through the air, and the orb accelerated heavenward at enormous speed.

Heading high into the sky, as bright as a meteor, the orb lit the landscape below it like a flare fired over no man's land.

As its momentum stalled, the orb made a graceful arc, before plummeting towards the ground, leaving behind it a trail of sparks, like the re-entry of a space shuttle through Earth's atmosphere.

"Oh no!" said Sergeant Spencer, his body rigid. "That's not good."

Silently agreeing with her father, Millie craned her neck to watch the orb through clouds of her own condensed, nervous breath.

Gathering momentum, the orb sped through the night sky, leaving a trail of gold and silver in its wake.

Millie watched it until it vanished into the trees on the mountainside below them. Then she watched in astonishment as a mushroom cloud of colour rose from the forest.

When the cloud of sparks fell earthward again, and no sign of the orb's impact remained, Sergeant Spencer cleared his throat. "Oh no," he said. "Something tells me that I should be concerned about that."

"It'll be fine, Dad," said Judith. "If anybody saw it, they'll think it's a firework. Or a meteor. If somebody is interested enough to spend a few hours searching for it, they won't find anything. Don't worry."

"But it was magic!" answered Sergeant Spencer, "anything could happen!"

"No," said Millie. "It was negative energy — there was no spell attached. As soon as it hit the ground, that was the end of it."

"Are you both sure?"

"We're sure," said Judith. "Don't worry about it. And I promise I won't use any more magic while we're in Scotland unless it's absolutely necessary."

"I promise, too," said Millie.

The tension leaving his shoulders, Sergeant Spencer nodded. "Okay," he said. "Let's forget about it. It's time to enjoy Christmas. I don't know about anybody else, but I'm starving, and I don't feel like cooking tonight. It's not even eight o'clock yet. Who fancies heading down to the pub Edna told us about? The footpath she mentioned is just over there. Does anybody fancy a walk through a snowy forest, followed by whiskey and a hot meal? It would be nice to meet some of the locals."

"Don't get too excited about meeting the locals," squawked Reuben, from a branch of the Christmas tree, his eyes reflecting the lights. "They'll be Scottish."

"Less of that attitude, Reuben," said Millie, giving her familiar a stern stare. "You're beginning to sound xenophobic, or at least very, very rude. I'm warning you — if you misbehave while we're at the pub, it will be the last thing you do! Do you understand?"

Reuben cocked his head. Then he closed his eyes. He pecked at his foot before looking at his witch. "I think so," he huffed.

Chapter 4

The powerful torch which Sergeant Spencer used to pick out the path ahead of them was helpful, but not absolutely necessary. Even though the trail followed a curving route down the mountain through a pine forest, enough moonlight filtered through the branches to illuminate the path, giving the snow a blueish hue.

Edna had promised that The Kilted Stag would serve them some of the best food they'd ever tasted, and that the walk down the mountain into town would provide them with some of the freshest air they'd ever experienced. As Millie pulled her scarf tight around her neck and watched her breath condensing in the cold air, she couldn't have agreed with the elderly witch more.

The air smelled of pine needles and the sweet scent of ozone, and she suspected that if she'd drunk from the little stream which flowed alongside the path over shelves of ice, she'd have tasted some of the cleanest water she'd ever tried.

The haunting hoot of an owl echoed across the mountainside, and Reuben ducked his head into the breast pocket of Millie's goose down jacket. "This place is awful!" he said. "It's full of creatures that would eat me at the drop of a hat! I've seen what those owls do when they catch their prey, and I'm not about to become its meal. You should have left me back in the cabin with the television, instead of bringing me along this path full of owls, golden eagles and bears!"

Snow crunched under Millie's boots, and the tip of her nose burned with cold. "There are golden eagles here, but I don't think they hunt at night. Yes, you should be nervous of the owls, but you do know there are no bears in this country?"

"Whatever!" came Reuben's muffled voice. "I'm just saying that right now, I consider the place we are in to be worse than the place I came from before I was put in the body of this cockatiel!"

Considering she'd been there and had almost lost her life while navigating the barren lands of the other dimension, Millie knew that what he'd said was demonstrably false. "Scotland is not worse than The Chaos," she snapped. "Do you really believe that being in a dimension populated by all manner of evil creatures is better than taking a beautiful moonlit walk down a Scottish mountain towards the warmth of a local pub?"

"I'm not saying anything more on the matter," said Reuben, peaking out of Millie's pocket. "It seems to me that you've sided completely with the people of Scotland and have turned against your familiar. So be it."

Spotting movement from the corner of her eye, Millie didn't reply. She stopped walking and stared into the gloom of the forest. "I saw something," she said.

"A bear!" screeched Reuben. "Or a beaver!"

"What did you see, Millie?" asked Sergeant Spencer, crunching his way through the snow towards her. His eyes shone. "A deer perhaps? I'd love to spot a stag."

"People," murmured Millie. "At least that's what it looked like. A couple of them, walking."

"Probably hunters," said Judith. "Edna warned us that we might hear gunshots."

"She also warned us that if we see hunters, we're to make ourselves known, so we're not mistaken for deer, and shot," said Sergeant Spencer, striding towards the edge of the forest. Pushing past the pine trees, releasing fragrant sweetness into the air, he shouted into the gloom. "Hello? Is anybody there?"

First, there was silence. Then came the sound of small branches been pushed aside as something made its way through the trees.

"Hello?" repeated Sergeant Spencer, peering into the undergrowth.

Then Millie saw movement again, further away to her left this time. She pointed. "Over there," she said. "I'm sure it's people."

Forcing a path past the spindly branches of a pine tree, Sergeant Spencer swept the bright beam of the torch from left to right as he trudged into the forest. Keeping close behind her father, Millie stepped into the trees, too, followed by her sister.

"I want to make sure we speak to them," said Sergeant Spencer. "We're going to be here for a few days. Edna's cabin is normally empty — if there are hunters in the area, they need to know that there are people around." He moved the torch in wider arcs. "Hello!"

Then Millie saw them through the thin branches. Standing still in a small clearing. Three of them, their shadows elongated in the beam of the torch. She pointed. "There!" she said. "People."

Changing direction, Sergeant Spencer pushed through the branches towards the area Millie had indicated. "Hello!"

With no answer forthcoming from the three people, Sergeant Spencer and his daughters pushed further into the forest, following the beam of light which picked out the shapes partially hidden by trees.

As they drew closer, Sergeant Spencer came to a halt as he pushed past the last tree that blocked his view. He laughed, turning to look at Millie. "There are your people," he chortled, pointing into the forest.

Stepping around her father, Millie stared at the spot that the beam of light illuminated. She tutted. "Snowmen?" she said.

"You said you saw people moving," said Reuben. "Are you trying to scare me?"

"No," said Millie, still convinced she'd seen movement. "I could have sworn I saw somebody. And we all heard the sound of snapping branches."

"I'm sure this forest is full of wildlife," said Judith. "Even during winter."

"Well," said Sergeant Spencer, approaching the three snow sculptures, each with pebbles forming crude mouths and eyes, their gnarly stick arms spread as if they were being crucified. "They're just snowmen, and judging by the lack of footprints around them, they're not fresh, so I don't think you saw the people who made them, Millie. If you saw movement, it was probably a deer or a fox."

"Oh, golly!" came Reuben's squeaking voice. "I'd forgotten about foxes!"

Frowning, Millie reluctantly nodded, convinced that what she'd seen had been people. "Yes," she said. "I must have seen an animal." She stared into the blank face of the nearest snowman. "Why would somebody build snowmen here? In the middle of a forest on a mountain?"

"Imagine being a child and living here," said

Sergeant Spencer, shining the torch into the face of a snowman with a particularly evil grimace. "Kids must have a wonderful life in these mountains, of course they'll be up here, exploring and enjoying the fresh air. And what kid doesn't like building a snowman?"

"I suppose so," said Millie.

"Now we know we're not going to get shot by hunters," said Judith, stomping her feet to keep warm. "Can we get to the pub? I'm starving, I wouldn't say no to a glass of wine or two either."

THE FOOTPATH EMERGED INTO THE LITTLE TOWN OF Kilgrettin alongside an old water mill built on the banks of a narrow river. With the roads and pavements cleared of snow, the walk down the hill into the town centre made Millie glad she'd come to Kilgrettin.

Christmas lights were strung around trees and bushes in people's gardens, and warm, welcoming light flooded from houses, turning the snow a golden colour.

Then, as she heard a Christmas carol wafting from a nearby house, and smelt baking pastry on the air, she felt it. Christmas cheer. She was well and truly in the mood for Christmas.

Glancing into the windows of shops as they passed, the three of them chatted happily. Spotting a shop which crafted kilts, Millie smiled as she imagined her father in one, and wondered if she should buy him one while they were in Scotland.

Running her gloved hand through the snow on the window ledge of a quaint book shop, she promised herself that one of her New Year's resolutions would be to begin reading again. She'd let her passion for the written word be snuffed out when she'd moved to Spellbinder Bay, and she missed holding a book above her face as she lay in bed.

They found The Kilted Stag where Edna had said they would. The jewel in the crown of the little market square, the pub sat opposite the town's Christmas tree which shimmered beneath the lights adorning its branches.

With a beer garden at the front of the property, populated by revellers who ignored the cold nip in the air, the pub teemed with activity.

Stepping inside the old building, still aware of the curious looks some of the people in the beer garden had cast in her and her family's direction, Millie unwrapped the scarf from her neck.

Her nose tingling as the temperature climbed from snowy cold to log fire warm, she followed her father and Judith through a door which opened into a cosy room alive with the hum of conversation and the beat of lively music.

Prising open her coat pocket, she glanced at her familiar. "Please be good, Reuben," she said. "I know you've got a habit of not being able to keep your mouth shut in public, but this is not Spellbinder Bay. There's no concealment spell here. Non-paranormal people will know something is odd if you say anything more than 'who's a pretty boy then?' But even that's off-limits, okay?"

No answer came from her pocket, and the bird gazed up at her defiantly.

"Reuben, do you understand?"

The little bird opened and closed his beak and shook his little head.

Millie sighed. "You can speak to answer my question."

With a cheeky wink, the cockatiel nodded. "I shall try my best to be on my best behaviour."

"Good enough," said Millie.

As the three of them made their way to a table near the log fire, the room fell silent as more and more people noticed their presence, until the only sounds were a clink of ice against glass and a stool scraping on the wooden floor.

Even the jukebox had fallen silent, and the man standing next to it licked his lips as he watched them pass.

Alcohol reddened faces looked at them, and an elderly man whispered something to the woman next to him. She nodded and watched the progress the newcomers made as they took their seats and removed their coats.

"It's like something out of a bad horror film," whispered Judith.

"It's damned rude, is what it is," said Sergeant Spencer. He looked around the room, his eyes landing on the portly man next to the jukebox. He raised an eyebrow as he draped his coat over the back of his seat. "Don't turn the music off for our sakes. I like the song that was playing."

Glowering, the man reached for the base of the jukebox. The speakers crackled and Shakin' Steven's burst into life again, immediately changing the atmosphere in the room.

Conversations resumed, and a man laughed loudly, and then swallowed a long gulp of the black liquid in his pint glass. Another man tossed a pork scratching to the old brown labrador at his feet. Its teeth making easy work of the hard snack, the dog gobbled it down and looked up at its owner, hoping for another.

Looking towards the bar, Millie noticed the two men standing there. One of them rested his boot on the brass foot rail at the base of the bar, and the other sat on a stool, his legs splayed. Both of them stared intently at Millie and her family, neither making an effort to hide the fact.

Then, a small middle-aged woman appeared from a door behind the bar. She barked at the disinterested young barman who stood gazing at the TV set on the wall. "Wake up, Francis!" she said, moving strands of fiery red hair from her face. "I asked you to change a barrel!"

Reluctantly dragging his eyes from the silent TV set, the young man trudged past the woman with a shrug of his skinny shoulders.

When he'd left the bar area, the woman glanced around, and her eyes locked with Millie's. Her lips curled into a friendly smile, and she called across the room, her accent broad and pleasant. "What can I get you? A drink? Something to eat?"

Before anybody could answer, the man standing at the bar pushed himself from his leaning position and stood tall. His brown eyes narrowed, and he spoke through a thick black beard, his voice gravelly and slurred. "Who are you three?"

"Don't be so abrupt, Angus!" chastised the little lady behind the bar. She made a playful swipe at him with the tea towel in her hand. "You're rude."

Angus grunted a reply and lifted his drink from the bar, the whisky glass lost in the giant hand. He took a sip. "I've been called worse, Maggie."

Offering an apologetic smile, Maggie picked up three menus from the bar and hurried towards the fireplace. She placed the menus on the table and gave another broad smile. "I'm sorry. Angus has had too many whiskeys. His tongue is looser than normal."

"That's okay," said Millie, noting that Angus and his friend continued to stare.

When the man sitting on the stool caught Millie's eyes, he raised himself from a seated position and stood alongside Angus, dwarfed by the other man's bulk. Wearing a checked shirt and jeans, his spindly limbs and pinched nose gave him the appearance of a headmaster trying out as a lumberjack. He scowled. "Do you have family here in Kilgrettin? Are you here for Christmas?"

"Dougal!" snapped Maggie. "Leave them alone. They're entitled to come into my pub without being asked a hundred questions."

"Och, Maggie!" said Dougal. "I'm just curious." He smiled at Millie. "No offence meant to you. We don't often see strangers at this time of year — with the roads blocked as they always are."

Millie returned the smile, the glow of the crackling fire warming her cheeks. "We're staying in one of our friend's properties. Edna Brockett. She owns a log cabin up on the mountainside. At the top of the footpath near the mill."

Her face animated, Maggie stared at Millie. "Edna Brockett? How is she? She hasn't been back in town for years. We thought perhaps she'd died. Some of the lads go up to the cabin every year to do some maintenance, but we really thought we'd never see her again!"

"Edna Brockett," said Dougal. "There's something about that woman. She's always made me feel a little nervous."

"That's because you never made an effort to get to know her," said Maggie. "Edna's a wonderful woman. I miss her." She gave the trio at the table a warm smile. "Please tell her that Maggie sends her blessings."

"We will," said Judith.

"When did you get to town?" grunted Angus.

"About an hour and a half ago," said Sergeant Spencer.

"An hour and a half ago?" said Angus, his eyes darkening. "Through that snow? What did you arrive in? A tractor? A bloody tank? Nothing can get past the snow on those roads."

"It was *longer* than an hour ago, Dad," said Millie, winking at her father. "It was just as the snow was getting really bad. We managed to get through before the roads became blocked."

"Of course," said Sergeant Spencer. "It's been a long day and a stressful drive — I'm not used to driving in snow like that. We don't get much snow where we're from."

"Aye," chortled Dougal. "You southern softies have it easy down there."

"It has its unique challenges," said Millie. "Just like everywhere does."

"Ignore him," said Maggie. "He's just teasing." She slid one of the menus towards Sergeant Spencer. "Like you said, you've had a stressful day — you must be hungry and thirsty." Turning her back to the men at the bar, she spoke in a lowered voice. "I'm very fond of Edna. I'm not sure how you know her, and I'm not going to ask, but a friend of hers is a friend of mine. Choose your food. It's on me. I won't accept a penny from you."

"There's no need to —" began Judith.

"Choose whatever you want," said Maggie, winking, before making her way back to the bar. "It's Christmas. Consider it a gift and an apology for those two drunkard's rudeness."

Watching Maggie as she crossed the room, Judith spoke quietly. "Does she know Edna's a witch?"

"I don't know," said Millie. "She did tell us to give Edna her blessings."

"Just make sure that neither of you says anything out of turn," said Sergeant Spencer, opening a leather-bound menu. "This is a small town. Maggie is probably just a good friend of Edna's."

"Or she's a witch herself," suggested Judith, staring across the room at the small lady hurrying through an arch into a back room.

"Definitely don't go saying things like *that*," growled Sergeant Spencer. "Forget about it. They're just friends. Now, we're all hungry and thirsty, and there are some very tempting meals on this menu."

Her father was right, and as Millie scanned the neatly handwritten list of food, she found herself torn between the Angus beef steak and a traditional Scottish meat pie.

As she weighed her options, a tinny voice sounded from her coat. "What is haggis exactly? I mean, I've heard of it, but what is it *exactly*?"

Millie glanced down at the little cockatiel, his head

peering out of her coat pocket, his coal-black eyes darting across the menu. "I think it's offal," replied Millie, keeping her voice low.

"Then why do people eat it, if it's so awful?" asked Reuben.

Judith giggled. "Offal. Not awful," she said.

"What's that?" asked Reuben. "Some sort of strange Scottish creature? Like a bagpipe?"

"Not quite," replied Sergeant Spencer, slamming his menu shut and placing it on the table. "It's organ meat. It's the heart, lungs, kidney — that sort of thing. They grind them up and put them inside the intestines of an animal. It's a bit like a big circular sausage, but with much more herbs and spices. It's very nice. It's very traditional."

"They do what?" said Reuben, his voice increasing in both tempo and volume. "They mince up the organs of creatures, and then put them inside stomachs, and then they eat it? And that macabre abomination is their traditional dish? I told you the Scottish people were savages, but you wouldn't listen!"

"Reuben, be quiet!" hissed Millie.

"I won't be silenced! The Scottish people are savages!" repeated Reuben, this time, his voice deeper and angrier. "I wish I'd never come to Scotland. I don't want to be around these heathens at Christmas time!"

Moving slowly, Angus turned to face the table. He wiped whiskey from his beard and stared at Sergeant Spencer. "Did I just hear you correctly, wee man? You think we're savages?" Pulling his shirt sleeves up to his elbows, exposing muscular forearms thick with hair, Angus strode towards the table, his teeth bared beneath his beard. "I'll show you savages!"

"Heathens, too!" called Dougal. "I heard him call us heathens, too!"

"Oh no," said Millie, the huge man approaching quickly. "This is all we need."

Chapter 5

As Angus stormed towards the table, his face a mask of fury, Millie got to her feet. "Wait!" she said. "There's been a misunderstanding. It wasn't my father who said that!"

"Then who the hell was it?" demanded Angus, towering over the table, staring down at Sergeant Spencer, who sat with a nonchalant look on his face, his arms crossed.

Millie faltered for a moment and then pointed at Judith. "It was her. She was telling us about a funny part of a TV show she watched. She was repeating it to us."

"That was a man's voice we heard," said Angus.

"I was putting on a man's voice," said Judith, gazing up at the tall man, batting her eyelids a little too freely. "The part in the show was said by a man. I'm sorry if I offended you. We think Scotland is a wonderful place." She gave a warm smile, her cheeks glowing. "Please forgive me."

Judith's charms melted Angus's anger as effectively as her magic had melted snow, and the tension dropped from his shoulders as he grunted. "Well, we treat women with respect in these parts." He glared at Sergeant Spencer, who appeared unnerved. "You're lucky. I've knocked the teeth clean out of the mouths of bigger men than you."

Uncrossing his arms, Sergeant Spencer got to his feet. A full head shorter than the big Scottish man, he was still no midget. "I can look after myself. I'm sure I'd have been okay."

"That sounds like fighting talk," said Angus. "Would you like to continue this conversation outside? Away from the ladies?"

Just then, Maggie hurried through the door behind the bar carrying a tray of clean glasses. "What's going on here?" she demanded. "Angus! What are you doing? Are you threatening my guests?"

"It was a misunderstanding, Maggie," said Angus. "I thought they were disrespecting us. It's been sorted out — I'm just making it quite clear to the gentleman that we don't tolerate fools in Kilgrettin."

"Get back here right now, Angus, and concentrate on your whiskey," said Maggie. "Otherwise I'll send for Sophie and ask her to take you home."

"Och," grunted Angus, turning his back to the table. "You leave Sophie out of this, Maggie."

"Then behave yourself," suggested Maggie. "Otherwise I'll be forced to ask your wife to make you behave."

Then, just as Angus placed an elbow on the bar and resumed his position over his whiskey glass, the bar door slammed open, and a shapely woman hurried across the room. "Angus!" she shouted.

"You already sent for her, Maggie?" said Angus, rolling his eyes.

"Of course not," replied Maggie.

Reaching Angus's side, Sophie grabbed him by the wrist. "You've got to come home! Someone's been snooping around — he's terrified the kids, and I think I know who it is!"

"Calm down, love," said Angus, looking into his wife's face. "Slow down, tell me what happened."

Bouncing on her toes, Sophie babbled her words, her accent thick. "The kids were watching television, and they saw him looking into the lounge. Writing things in a little notebook. Probably taking note of what he can come back and steal while we're all asleep. He's probably after all the presents under the tree!"

"Who?" demanded Angus. "Who did the kids see? Are they okay?"

"The bairns are fine. Katie came round to watch them while I came to get you. I'll give you one clue as to who it was looking through our window, though," said Sophie. "He had a beard. A white beard."

The bar top shuddering as he slammed a ham-sized fist into it, Angus growled. "Christoph," he murmured. "Up to his thieving tricks again. That man shouldn't have come back to this town after being released from jail. I knew two months in the big-house couldn't rehabilitate a burglar like him. That's it, I'm going up to that little farm of his, and when I get hold of him — he'll regret ever choosing my house as a target for his dirty crimes!"

"I'll come with you," said Dougal. "He needs to be taught a lesson."

"Come on, boys," said Maggie. "Don't go doing anything silly. You don't know if he's done anything wrong yet. You should wait until you can let the police talk to him."

Angus shook his head. "Och, you know the police won't be able to get through for at least another two weeks. And they're not going to come all the way out here just because my kids thought they saw somebody peering in at the window. This is down to us. This is our town, and I won't have people in it who don't respect other people's property."

Downing the last inch of his whiskey, Dougal slammed his empty glass on the bar. "Me too. Come on, let's go and teach that thieving scum bag a lesson."

As the men made their way towards the door, with Sophie hurrying after them, Sergeant Spencer called out. "Wait there, gentlemen! Don't be so rash!"

Angus came to an abrupt halt and turned slowly on the spot. "Who the heck do you think you are? Don't you tell us what to do."

Reaching into his pocket, Sergeant Spencer withdrew his wallet and opened it to display his police badge. "I'm a Police Sergeant. My daughter's work for the police, too. I might not be a member of the Scottish Police Force, but I'm certain that they'd appreciate my help in this matter."

"We don't need your help, copper," snarled Angus. "I'm not even sure you have any jurisdiction in Scotland."

"Listen," replied Sergeant Spencer. "I've seen plenty of well-intentioned hotheads like you two being sent to prison because they didn't think things through before they acted. The man you *think* was looking into your window, might have been, but what if he wasn't? If you threaten him, he's going to say he didn't do anything, even if he did. It's going to end in violence. Maybe an innocent man is going to get hurt. It will end up with you two in prison. It's not worth it."

"Maybe you do things differently down south," said Angus. "But we're not the type of people who tolerate men sneaking around our town, peering into our homes. Especially men who have already been to prison for breaking into houses."

"You don't know if it was him," said Sergeant Spencer.

"Are you calling my kids, liars?" shouted Sophie. "My kids know what they saw. They saw a man with a white beard looking through our lounge window."

"I'm not saying your children are lying," said Sergeant Spencer. "What I am saying is that you're concentrating on the fact that the person they saw has a white beard. I'm sure there are plenty of people with white beards. Look around this pub, there are three men in here with white beards."

As everybody in the pub watched the disturbance with interest, one of the men sporting a white beard shuffled nervously in his seat. "It wasn't me!" he said. "I've been here all day!"

"We know it wasn't you, Ken," said Angus. "You're one of us. You're not like Christoph."

Sergeant Spencer stepped away from his seat and grabbed his coat. "Let us come with you. You'll discover that a police badge extracts the truth a lot more effectively than threats of violence do."

Angus remained quiet for a few seconds, and then his shoulders slumped. He nodded. "Okay," he grunted. "Let's do it your way." He paused for a few seconds and then looked up. "To begin with."

He kissed his wife. "You go home to the kids. I'll be home when I've made sure Kilgrettin will be free from thieves tonight."

Chapter 6

Having suggested that as he was sober, he should drive the old pick-up truck belonging to Dougal, neither of the Scottish men argued with Sergeant Spencer as they squeezed onto the double passenger seat. Both men appeared to understand that driving under the influence of alcohol in front of a police officer was not a great idea, even if that policeman was from the South of England.

As the clunky vehicle rattled along dark country lanes, heading out of town, Millie peered into her pocket. "You'd better not mess up again," she warned. "Or I'll cut the plug off the TV."

Nodding quickly, his eyes panicked, Reuben spoke in a whisper. "I'll be good. You won't hear a peep from me."

Following Angus's barked directions, Sergeant Spencer turned right into a narrow lane, the headlights picking out a fox skulking into the thin winter hedgerow.

Ploughing through knee-high snow, the pick-up bounced along the potholed road on broken suspension. Then the lights of a house appeared around a bend, and a minute later they arrived at a smallholding located on the lower slopes of a mountain.

The headlights illuminating a handful of outhouses and barns, Sergeant Spencer brought the vehicle to a halt next to a snow-covered car parked outside the house, the door of which stood wide open.

Angus climbed from the vehicle first. He rushed towards the house, stepping into the light spilling from the open doorway onto icy cobbles. The wind lifted powdered snow and blew little clouds of it through the open door into the hallway, and the sound of a television blared from somewhere within the property.

"Wait there!" shouted Sergeant Spencer as Angus stepped over the threshold. "You can't just rush in. It's against the law."

"The bloody law!" said Angus, shaking his head, but taking a step back into the cold air. "The law is only there for those that don't obey it. It seems like they get away with anything, while we law-abiding citizens have to pick up the mess after them."

"Nevertheless," said Sergeant Spencer, making his way towards the door. "We all have to abide by it." Having said that, he made a fist and leaning through the doorway, he knocked on the door and looked at Angus. "What's the gentleman's full name?"

"Christoph," said Angus. "Christoph Gruber."

Sergeant Spencer banged on the door once more. "Mister Gruber," he shouted. "Mister Gruber. It's the police. Could you come to the door, please?"

"I've got a feeling something's not right," said Millie. "Something feels off."

"What are you, some sort of psychic?" laughed Dougal.

Millie looked at him and narrowed her eyes. "Not quite," she said. "But maybe I can tell what you're thinking."

Looking uncomfortable, Dougal blinked once or twice, then looked away, hiding his face.

Knocking on the door again, Sergeant Spencer took a step into the house. "Mr Gruber, we're coming in. We'd like to ask you some questions about something that happened in town."

Traipsing through the brightly lit hallway, Sergeant Spencer headed for the room from which the sounds of the TV emanated. A sparsely decorated Christmas tree stood at an odd angle in the corner, and a single Christmas card had been propped up on the mantelpiece.

A fire roared in the hearth, and Millie guessed it couldn't have been lit more than half an hour ago. An open newspaper lay on the sofa, alongside a plate with a slice of what looked like fruit cake on it.

A dining table stood against one of the walls, and on it was the cake from which the piece on the settee had been cut.

Suddenly, taking on the role of detective rather than hothead, Angus turned the TV volume down and surveyed his surroundings. "A piece of stollen that looks like the first piece from a freshly baked cake. A roaring fire. And a newspaper open on the sports page — I have a feeling that Christoph is preparing for a cosy night in. Perhaps he's in the bathroom."

"Stollen?" came a small voice from Millie's pocket. "What's stollen?"

Angus answered, assuming it had been Millie who'd asked the question. "It's a fruit loaf. It's German or Austrian, I'm not sure which. There's lots of fruit and marzipan in it. It's pretty tasty."

"Aye," said Dougal. "Christoph is Austrian. He moved to Kilgrettin twenty years ago."

Judith appeared in the doorway. "I've been upstairs. He's not there."

"Well, it looks like he was about to read the sports page and eat a slice of cake in front of the fire," said Sergeant Spencer. "He must be here."

"He keeps animals outside," said Dougal. "A cow in the barn, and a few pigs in the shed. Maybe he's gone to check on them."

Stepping outside again, Millie scanned the courtyard for movement. Snow had already covered the footsteps they'd left as they'd walked from the car to the house, so there was no chance of Christoph's footprints being visible.

"Mr Gruber!" shouted Sergeant Spencer. When no answer came, his face belied his anxiety. "I agree with Millie. Something feels off. I've been a policeman long enough to pick up on these things. Let's have a look around."

As Millie walked towards a small outhouse, the sloping roof thick with snow, she noticed Angus through the gloom, and came to a halt, staring at him.

Barely visible in the shadow of a large barn, with his face tilted towards the sky, the big man appeared to be sniffing the air. His nostrils twitched, and he moved his face from side to side as if searching out a scent.

Then, he stepped out of the shadows and strode quickly and confidently towards the open gate of a field. He stood knee-deep in snow and stared into the whiteness, sniffing the air again, this time making it less obvious to a casual observer.

Suddenly, he swivelled his head and stared directly at Millie. Then he stared at the snow in the field as if looking for footprints. "I think he went this way," he shouted. "I think I see something."

Not waiting for anybody to join him, Angus ran into the field, the darkness swallowing him. Millie hurried after him, cold biting at her nose. Trying to step in the large footprints Angus had left in the snow, her legs proving to be too short, Millie ploughed her own route through the field. Then she heard Angus shout. "I've found him. He needs help!"

The snow making it hard to move fast, Millie pushed forward. Then, as the moon slid from behind a cloud, she saw Angus.

Crouching in the snow, he looked up as Millie approached. "Prepare yourself. It's not a pretty sight, but he's got a pulse. It's faint, but it's there. We need to get him into town right away."

Hearing shouting voices behind her as the others approached, Millie stared into the snow at Angus's feet.

At first, it was hard to understand what she was looking at. She could tell that it was a man, naked from the waist up, lying face down in the snow — but the smudges of darkness on his back confused her. Then, as more moonlit illuminated the gruesome scene, she knew what she was seeing.

Criss-crossed with wounds, from which blood trickled into the snow around him, the thin man's back was a mangled mess of gashes. "Poor man," she said. "Are you sure he's alive?"

"For now," said Angus, getting to his feet.

"Oh no!" said Judith, arriving with Sergeant Spencer and Dougal. She put a hand to her mouth as she stared at the bloody mess. "What happened to him?"

"He's alive," said Millie, getting to her feet. "But he needs a hospital."

His face whiter than the snow surrounding them, Dougal spoke quietly. "What are those marks?"

Crouching next to the injured man, Sergeant Spencer placed his fingers on Christoph's throat and felt for a pulse. Then he looked up at Dougal, anger in his eyes. "It looks like somebody got to him and did what you two wanted to do. This is what happens when hotheads are allowed to take the law into their own hands." He stood up and stared into the dark. "Where do we take him? We can't get to a hospital with all that snow on the roads."

"There's a well-stocked and equipped medical centre in town," said Dougal. "It's set up like a mini-hospital. We have a doctor and some nurses who live in Kilgrettin."

Taking his coat off, and laying it over the man in the snow, Sergeant Spencer looked at Angus. "You grab his legs. I'll grab his arms. Dougal, you take the weight in the middle. His pulse is weak, and he's freezing. If we don't get him to that medical centre, I don't think he'll last an hour."

Chapter 7

By the time they'd arrived at the medical centre, housed in what was once a chapel, Christoph Gruber's condition had deteriorated further. His pulse fluttered erratically against Millie's fingers, and his breathing had become barely detectable. As Angus and her father lifted the man from the vehicle, she doubted he would see Christmas Day.

The plump nurse on duty, who'd been concentrating on a television screen when they'd burst through the door with Christoph, gave a horrified shriek, but then, to her credit, rose to the occasion. "Somebody run to the Highland Hotel and get the doctor," she ordered, piercing the skin on the back of Christoph's hand with a cannula. "He's attending a dinner party."

"I'll go," said Dougal, hurrying for the door, his face pale beneath the sterile light.

When Dougal had left, Angus stood quietly in the corner, his eyes flitting between the injured man on the bed, and the floor.

Millie studied him, wondering if her suspicions were correct. She'd seen him sniffing the air, and she'd watched him lead them straight to an injured man lying in deep snow in a dark field.

Was he a werewolf? She couldn't be sure, and she wasn't about to ask. If he wasn't a werewolf, he'd think Millie was mad, and if he was, it was none of Millie's business.

As the nurse worked, Millie, Judith and Sergeant Spencer gave her the space she required, watching as she inserted a tube down Christoph's throat. She attached numerous wires to his chest and stomach and checked his blood pressure.

When she'd finished stabilising him, she began working on his wounds. As she did, Sergeant Spencer photographed them with his mobile. Evidence that might be required at a later date.

By the time the doctor burst in, looking a little unsteady on his feet, the nurse had done most of the work. Her hand trembled as she stepped away from the bed. "I wasn't expecting that tonight," she said, a tremble in her voice as well as her hand.

"We've both seen things we didn't expect to see tonight," said the doctor, the sweet scent of alcohol pouring off him as he spoke. "Nobody would believe me if I told them what I'd seen tonight. I'm not even sure I believe it myself, and I saw it with my own two eyes."

Raising an eyebrow in Millie's direction, Sergeant Spencer placed a hand on the doctor's back. "I don't mean to be rude, Doctor, but I'm a Police Sergeant, and where I come from there are rules and regulations that say a medical professional should not be under the influence of alcohol when he or she work on a patient. I'm sure you have the same rules and regulations here in Scotland."

The doctor, a middle-aged man with an extra chin, and eyebrows which almost met in the middle, stood up straight and stared at Sergeant Spencer. "Of course there are rules and regulations," he said. "And of course we'd all like to abide by them. I wasn't supposed to be on duty tonight, Sergeant. I was supposed to be enjoying a dinner party hosted by the Hunting Lodge, but instead, I've seen things tonight which I can't quite understand, and now I find myself here, tending to a gentleman who would have died had you not brought him here when you did." He took a deep breath and pinched the bridge of his nose between finger and thumb.

"He was lucky that we found him," said Millie. She looked at Angus. "It was lucky that Angus found him."

The doctor nodded. "Quite frankly, I'm not in a fit state to be treating this gentleman, but I happen to be the only doctor in a tiny Highland town, currently cut off from the rest of the world by deep snow. I rarely drink. In fact, the last time I took a drink was at a barbecue during the summer.

“Maybe it's complacency on our behalf, but we don't expect emergencies such as this to arrive at the medical centre. As you will have noticed, Nurse Tomlinson is extremely adept at what she does, and thanks to her, there is nothing that I need to do under the influence of alcohol. Mister Gruber is in a coma and has been made as comfortable as possible. I'll be sober in a few hours, and then I shall spend my Christmas ensuring he survives. I will not apologise for the fact that I've taken a drink tonight. I hope you'll understand."

"Of course," said Sergeant Spencer. "Of course. I'm sorry, I didn't mean to insinuate anything."

"Will he live?" asked Angus.

"There's no way of telling yet," said the doctor. "We'll know more tomorrow, but for now, I suggest you all go home."

Angus cleared his throat. He approached Sergeant Spencer. "You know me and Dougal didn't do this, right? You were in the pub when my wife came in to tell me that somebody had been looking through the window. Only then did we go to Christoph's home. You were with us — you know it wasn't us?"

"I know," said Sergeant Spencer. "But rest assured, until the Scottish Police can get through the snow, I’m going to try my best to find out who did this."

Angus nodded. Then he walked to the door. “Goodnight,” he said, leaving the room.

When the door had swung shut behind him, the doctor shook his head. "I wouldn't waste your time trying to solve any mysteries around here," he said. "People around these parts won't talk to police in general, and especially to outsiders. They like to do things their own way. I've never seen you before, so I'm assuming you're here for Christmas — if I were you, I'd do just that — enjoy your Christmas and let the Scottish Police try and solve this one when the snow clears."

"I can't promise anything," said Sergeant Spencer. "My daughters and I are staying in the log cabin up on the hill. Owned by a lady named Edna Brockett."

"I know it," said the doctor.

"If he does regain consciousness, I'd appreciate it if you would contact me. I'd like to ask him some questions. Even if I can't solve this crime, I can pass on any information I get from him to the Scottish police," said Sergeant Spencer.

The doctor nodded. "We'll let you know if his condition changes."

As the father and daughters left the room, Judith looked back at the doctor. "I hope you don't mind me asking, but you mentioned you'd seen something tonight that you couldn't explain. I wondered what it was."

"It's silly," said the doctor. "You wouldn't believe me. But I know what I saw."

"We're pretty open-minded," said Millie. "Try us."

"I'm quite interested too, Doctor," said Nurse

Tomlinson. "And you know how much I trust you. I'll believe you."

The doctor took a deep breath. He straightened his tie, and then he puffed out his chest. As the machine Christoph was attached to beeped in the background, the doctor closed his eyes for a moment and then spoke. "Earlier tonight, I saw what can only be described as Santa Claus. Not the Santa Claus who stands outside the convenience store every Christmas collecting money for orphaned children. Not the Santa Claus who the children visit in the grotto next to the church. I mean, I saw Santa."

He lifted a single finger and pointed towards the ceiling. "I saw him up there. Flying. As plain as I can see all of you now. I saw his sleigh, bright red, soaring through the night sky. I watched him circling the town, and then I watched him vanish into the distance. Then, I promised myself I would never speak of what I'd seen to anybody. When I finish telling you, I would like none of you to say a word. I'm happy that I've been able to share my experience with somebody. You can all chalk it down to a man not used to drinking alcohol, partaking in a little too much and seeing things that weren't there — I don't mind what you think. I know what I saw, and nothing will ever dissuade me. Now, I think you should leave. Myself and Nurse Tomlinson have work to do."

As she stepped outside the medical centre into the cold night air, Millie looked at her father and then her sister. "You know what he saw, don't you?"

"Yes," said Sergeant Spencer. "And that's why we shouldn't use magic where there's no concealment spell to hide it. That poor man believes he saw Santa. He's always going to believe that. Can you imagine how much his life might change because of this? There's to be no more magic until we're back in Spellbinder Bay, and we may have to ask Henry Pinkerton to wipe the poor man's memory of the incident."

"No more magic," agreed Millie.

"No more magic," said Judith.

"What's happening?" came a little voice from Millie's coat pocket. "I fell asleep when I discovered what stollen was. I dreamed of marzipan. I was very tired. Have I missed anything?"

"You've missed a little," said Millie. "Let's go back to the cabin and have something to eat. We'll fill you in on the details while we walk back up that mountain."

Chapter 8

Millie couldn't remember the last time she'd been woken up by people singing Happy Birthday to her.

She sat up in bed, the fluffy duvet soft against her skin, feeling utterly refreshed after an excellent night's sleep.

The beds in the cabin were of very high quality — her father had said they were handcrafted, and the mattress and pillows had made Millie feel like she'd been sleeping on a cloud.

She smiled at her family, who were singing the last warbled notes of the traditional birthday song. Reuben sat on Judith's shoulder, his head cocked to the side, his chest swelling as he whistled the tune accompanying the not so harmonious father and daughter duet.

When the song came to an end, and Judith bent down to hug her sister, Millie gave a big smile.

"Thank you! Thank you all," she said. "I couldn't have asked for a better way to have been woken up today."

"Do you feel any older, Millie?" asked Reuben. "How old are you today? Twenty-nine? Thirty-two? Forty-four?"

"She's twenty-six, Reuben," said Sergeant Spencer. "And this is the first birthday I've spent with her." Wiping a finger beneath his eye, he bent down and gripped Millie in a fierce hug. "Happy birthday, darling," he said. "I'm so proud of you. I love you so much."

Holding her tears back, Millie kissed her father on the cheek, enjoying the spicy scent of his aftershave. "Thank you, Dad," she said.

"Your presents are waiting for you in the lounge," said Judith.

"And they've made a surprise breakfast for you," blurted Reuben. "But I'm not allowed to eat any until you're out of bed. So, please get up, birthday girl!"

"Reuben!" said Judith. "It was called a surprise breakfast because it was supposed to be a surprise."

Not wanting to tell them she'd already smelt bacon cooking, she did wonder where it had come from. They'd brought with them non-perishables such as coffee and sugar, and a bag full of convenience food. They hadn't packed any food that needed refrigerating, and they hadn't had time to visit any shops in Kilgrettin.

When they'd got back to the cabin the night

before, they'd rummaged through the supplies they'd brought and had ended up eating crackers and peanut butter.

She sniffed the air, pretending she'd only just noticed the tempting scent of bacon. "That's a nice smell — I didn't know we had bacon here."

"We didn't," said Judith. "Dad took a walk down the mountain to see how Christoph is doing. The little grocery store which couples as a newsagent opens early."

"And a lovely walk it was, too," smiled Sergeant Spencer. He took an over exaggerated deep breath. "I've never experienced air so fresh. It actually makes me want to exercise more."

"Well," said Millie, "it might encourage you to continue with an exercise routine when we get home."

"I wouldn't wish too hard for that," said Sergeant Spencer. "Because I don't think it's going to come true! Oh, and guess what — there are more snowmen. Some kids must've built them early this morning. There are some on the path, and some just in the edge of the tree line. The kids who built them are really embracing the Christmas spirit."

"And Christoph?" asked Millie. "How is he?"

"He's doing remarkably well," said her father. "The doctor says his wounds aren't as bad as they looked and that most of his problems stemmed from hypothermia. He expects him to wake later today."

"Then we'll go and ask him some questions," said Judith.

"But without getting too involved in the case," said Sergeant Spencer. "I've been thinking. We're here for Christmas, not to find out who beat Christoph Gruber. We'll investigate any information that comes our way, but that will be the extent of our involvement. We'll gather just enough information to pass on to the Scottish Police Force, and then try and put it from our minds."

"Sounds good to me," said Millie. *It did.* Since moving to Spellbinder Bay, she'd helped solve several crimes, and she didn't want her Christmas break away from the murder ridden town to be tainted by yet another investigation. Not that she disliked bringing people to justice, but she hadn't come all the way to Scotland to solve crimes. She'd come to celebrate.

"So, Millie," said Reuben, fluttering from Judith's shoulder and landing on the bed. "Are you going to get up? You know you said the bacon *smells* nice? Well, I've *seen* it, and I'd very much like to get a taste of it. So, if you don't mind — please get out of bed."

"Okay," smiled Millie. "If you get out of my room, I'll get ready."

Dragging herself from beneath the hot water streaming from the large shower head had proved quite difficult, but knowing people were waiting for her, she'd pulled herself away from the view across the snowy valley, and the floral notes of her favourite shower gel.

After giving her hair a half-hearted blast of hot air, she tied it in a ponytail and opened her suitcase. Then she sighed, and got dressed in her pyjamas.

"Reuben!" she yelled. "Come here!"

Summoned by his witch, the little bird had no choice but to get to her side as quickly as possible. Had his duty as a familiar not been enforced by magic, Millie doubted he would have come so willingly. She opened the door and stared at him as he fluttered in and landed on the chest of drawers. Her heart softening, she already knew that she couldn't be angry with the little bird. "What did you put in my suitcase, Reuben?"

The cockatiel stared at his feet and mumbled something.

"Pardon?" said Millie. "Speak up. I can't hear you. What did you put in my suitcase?"

"Ice-cream," muttered Reuben. "I put ice-cream in, and a half-eaten jam doughnut. I couldn't let Judith get away with removing them, Millie. I really wanted to bring them with me! I didn't ask to bring anything else! They were my Desert Island Disc luxury items. Please don't be angry."

Millie stared at the mess in her suitcase, then she looked at her familiar. "I'm not angry. It's my birthday today, and Christmas Day tomorrow. Of course I'm not angry — I'm happy to be surrounded by such a lovely family."

"Will you use magic to clean your clothes?" asked Reuben, perking up.

Millie shook her head. "No. There's to be no more magic."

"But the Christmas tree that you and Judith used magic to decorate is still decorated," said Reuben. "That's magic."

"That's residual magic," said Millie. "It can't harm anybody, and nobody will know any different. It's almost like an illusion."

"What will you wear?" said Reuben. "Have I ruined all your clothes?"

"I'll wear my pyjamas until my clothes have been washed and dried."

"Good!" said Reuben. "Is my ice-cream salvageable? I'm not so concerned about the doughnut."

"I'm afraid not," said Millie. "But I'll get some for you today when we go shopping."

As she entered the lounge, her eyes were automatically drawn to the beautifully decorated Christmas tree standing proud in the corner. Then, she took in the garlands hanging on the mantelpiece, and the little Christmas ornaments that were scattered across shelves and cupboards. "Wow!" she said. "You decorated! It looks fantastic!"

"I know you like to help with the decorations," said Judith. "But Dad and I thought we'd do it last night after you'd gone to bed. We thought it would be a nice surprise."

"I had to be very quiet when I cut down the tree,"

laughed Sergeant Spencer. "Judith kept hissing at me. Telling me I was going to wake you up."

Giving her sister a kiss first, and then her father, Millie felt a sudden rush of warm happiness running through her. "Now it feels Christmassy!"

"It's your birthday first," said Judith. She reached for a present, the wrapping a gold paper which crinkled enticingly as she passed it to her sister. "Happy birthday!"

"Thank you!" said Millie, her nostrils under assault from the heavenly aromas of strong coffee and bacon. She smiled at her sister as she began picking at the neatly tied ribbon.

"You're still in your pyjamas," noted Judith. "Expecting a lazy birthday, are you?"

"Not quite," said Millie, tugging gently at a corner of the paper, not wanting to ruin Judith's beautiful wrapping. "Let's just say that Reuben is very good at hiding contraband."

Judith's face remained blank for a few seconds, and then she wagged a finger at the cockatiel. "You sneaked the ice-cream back into her suitcase!"

The feathers on the bird's chest ruffled as he puffed out his chest. "I did indeed, Judith," he boasted. "I did, indeed. The doughnut, too."

Judith's face brightened as Millie peeled back a piece of sticky tape and folded open the wrapping paper. "For the first time in my life, I might have bought a present that somebody actually needs!"

Her fingers brushing soft material as she peeled

back more of the paper, Millie smiled. She removed the last of the wrapping and grinned as she held a gift in each hand. "Jeans and a sweater!"

Placing the folded jeans on a chair, she allowed the sweater to unfurl and laughed as she studied the motif knitted into the strands of colourful wool. The words, *It's my birthday, and I'll fly if I want to,* were written in bold letters around the image of a shapely young witch perched on a broomstick, a big smile on her face and a cupcake, pierced with a single candle, in her hand.

Slipping the sweater over her pyjama top, Millie hugged her sister. "Thank you! I love it!"

"When I chose it, I had no idea you'd have actually learned how to fly when you opened it," said Judith. "It's far more poignant than when I bought it!"

"And don't get any more ideas about turning that car into an aircraft," said Sergeant Spencer. "That sweater is not to be taken seriously!" With a twinkle in his eye, he handed Millie a neatly wrapped package, his smile communicating a wealth of emotion. "Happy birthday, Millie," he said.

Beneath the paper, Millie found a small black box. She opened it gingerly, holding her breath as the hinged lid lifted. The pendant twinkled in the cold winter light, and she bit her lip as she lifted the delicate chain and examined the necklace. "It's…beautiful," she murmured, captivated by the light which bounced from the stone in the centre of the silver pendant. Then she noticed the smaller stones surrounding it, twinkling like the stars she'd seen in the Scottish night sky.

"It's Blue Zircon," said her father. "It's your birthstone, Millie. And the little stones around it are diamond chips. Twenty-five of them. One for each of your birthdays that I missed."

Her eyes swimming with tears, Millie lifted her ponytail as her father placed the silver chain around her neck. Then, when the pendant pressed gently against her skin, she opened her arms and gripped both her father and sister in a tight hug. "Thank you," she said. "Both of you." She glanced towards Reuben who sat on a kitchen stool, staring into the oven, from which wafted mouthwatering aromas. "You, too, Reuben. Thank you for being my friend."

"You're welcome," replied the bird. "Can we eat yet?"

"Yes," said Sergeant Spencer, kissing each of his daughters on the forehead before striding towards the kitchen. "Let's eat. You two put your coats on and go outside. I'll bring breakfast."

"Outside?" asked Millie.

"There's a picnic bench out there," said Judith, wriggling into her coat. "We didn't see it last night in the dark. It's near the Christmas tree you and I decorated — it's got the most amazing views!"

With a clear blue sky and a warm sun, Mother Nature had gifted Millie the most beautiful day on which to celebrate her birthday. Following Judith to the little table that sat alongside the cabin, she stared in awe at the view.

The landscape had been lovely when lit by moonlight. But now, sparkling in the bright winter sun, it was capable of taking breath away.

Mountains soared into the sky, snow-covered and misty. Through a tree-lined gap between two of the tallest peaks, the eye was able to travel for miles across snowy lowlands which would eventually meet the ocean.

A tiny robin with a bright red breast and shiny eyes perched on a branch of the magically decorated Christmas tree. Its tiny head cocked, it watched with interest as Millie and Judith cleared snow from the benches and table.

They sat next to each other and gazed across the valley — two sisters enjoying a moment of peaceful tranquillity.

Landing on the table, his feet leaving prints in the thin dusting of snow which remained, Reuben studied the robin with suspicion. "What's he after?"

"Probably food," said Millie. "Robins are quite brave. They'll approach people a lot more readily than other wild birds will."

"After food?" he screeched, launching himself from the table and flying the short distance to the Christmas tree. He landed on the branch alongside the robin, shaking snow from the tree as he did.

The little robin seemed unperturbed, stepping a

few inches to the left and studying Reuben with curiosity.

Moving closer to the smaller bird, Reuben glared at it. "You listen to me, you feathery little freak. You might think you can parade around with that pretty little breast of yours, tricking people into giving you scraps of food. But you won't get away with it while I'm here! I'll be having all the scraps! You can scavenge in the snow beneath the table for crumbs when I've finished — or eat seeds and worms like the other commoners! You make sure you keep your distance, or you'll see the wrath of a cockatiel!"

The little robin tilted his head and looked up at Reuben. Then he whistled a short tune, his little eyes reflecting sunlight.

"Don't be so cruel," said Judith. "There'll be plenty of food for us all, including that poor little thing. It's freezing cold, and the ground is hard so it can't get to the worms. Do you want to be responsible for it starving to death, Reuben, because you were too greedy to allow it a few bacon rinds?"

"One phrase," remarked Reuben, studying Judith. "Survival of the fittest. Natural selection."

"I hate to disappoint you," said Millie. "But you are not the result of natural selection, Reuben. You're a demon from another dimension placed in the body of a cockatiel. Had you been a normal cockatiel, I think you'd have frozen to death by now. You have magic protecting you — that poor little fellow relies on the kindness of people."

Wagging a judgemental finger at the cockatiel, Judith frowned. "And hopefully, the kindness of its fellow birds."

"Kindness, be damned!" said Reuben, fluttering back to the table, having given the robin one last warning stare. "When I've eaten my fill, Mister Show-off over there can have the scraps."

Boots crunched through snow, and Sergeant Spencer approached the table. "Here we go!" he said, carrying a heavily laden tray. His breath condensing in the air, he placed the tray on the table and smiled proudly at his daughters. "A pot of tea," he said, pointing at the spout of the teapot protruding from a tartan tea-cosy. A small pot of coffee for you, Millie. Bacon, black pudding, sausage — of the square Scottish variety. Eggs — fried, of course. And on this plate, we have French toast, fried in bacon fat, and of course, one bowl of baked beans and a bowl of mushrooms."

As her father sat down, a grin still on his face, Millie took a mug from the tray and poured herself a coffee. Without a shot of caffeine in her veins, no day ever felt like it had truly begun. She swallowed the hot liquid. "This is amazing, Dad," she said. "And what a place to eat it. Just look at that view!"

"I'm glad you like it," said Sergeant Spencer. "Happy birthday."

Loading their plates with food, the three of them tucked into their breakfasts. Their breath left little clouds in the air as they ate, and the clink of cutlery on porcelain echoed through the surrounding forest.

As Millie bit into a piece of crispy bacon, a small dribble of fat escaped over her lip and headed for the little cleft in her chin. Watching her family eating, she gave silent thanks once more to the fact that she'd found her father and sister.

She cut into her square sausage, the glorious scent of herbs and spices rising to her nostrils. She dipped a piece into the bright orange yolk of an egg, which her father had explained was organic and pastured.

Fatty and satisfying, the eggs were undoubtedly tastier than the ones she was used to, and she closed her eyes in pleasure as rich, creamy yolk and spicy sausage coated her tongue.

Swallowing the piece of French toast which had been used to wipe her plate clean, she washed her meal down with another cup of steaming black coffee. Giving a contented sigh, she watched Reuben pecking at a piece of sausage on the little plate she'd given him.

With a suspicious eye on the robin, which had sidled along the branch it perched on, Reuben continued to eat pieces of sausage and bacon, his beak shining with fat.

When the robin gave a little chirp, Reuben shook his head as if exasperated. "I'm trying to eat in peace," he murmured.

The robin chirped again, this time leaping from the tree branch and fluttering on tiny wings to the table. Perching on the very edge, its little feet gripping the wood, it stared around the table with trusting eyes.

Keeping still, Millie, Judith and their father watched in fascination as the robin placed his trust in them, and took a dainty step closer towards Reuben and the plate he fed from.

"Oh, for heaven's sake!" squawked Reuben. "Talk about making me feel guilty!" He gave a frustrated shake of his head, and then tossed a bacon rind in the direction of the robin.

The little robin made a happy chirruping sound and set about attacking the rind as if it hadn't eaten for days.

"You're hungry, little fellow," said Reuben, his voice softer. "Here, have some sausage."

Its body language reflecting the fact that it trusted the humans at the table, the brightly coloured bird hopped closer to the plate. Soon, it was eating alongside Reuben, both birds eyeing each other as they shared their meal.

"Have as much as you like," said Reuben. "There's plenty to go around."

"You've changed your tune, Reuben," said Millie. "What about survival of the fittest?"

"I sense a kind heart in this little chap," said Reuben. "I like him. He needs a name. I know — I shall call him Robin."

"That must have taken a lot of brainpower to come up with, Reuben," chortled Sergeant Spencer, wiping his mouth with a paper serviette.

Just then, their attention was drawn by the sound of a roaring engine approaching. As one, the three of them looked along the track which led from the main road to the log cabin, still inaccessible due to snow.

Then, with engine smoke trailing behind it, and a massive snow ploughing blade fitted to the front, a tractor appeared, its blue paintwork bright in the winter landscape.

"We've got company," said Sergeant Spencer.

Chapter 9

"Who is it?" asked Judith, shielding her eyes from the sun.

"I'm not sure," said Sergeant Spencer, getting to his feet. "But it looks like whoever it is, they're doing us a favour."

The blade made easy work of the snow, pushing it aside into steep banks that formed walls alongside the track. It moved far more quickly through the snow than Millie would have imagined, and in less than two minutes, it was at the cabin.

With sunlight reflecting off the windows, it was hard to see the driver, but as she squinted against the bright light, Millie recognised the man at the wheel. "It's Angus," she said, noting his impressive beard and dark eyes.

"He might be here with news about Christoph," suggested Sergeant Spencer.

The tractor engine stopped with a rattle, and

Angus stepped down from the high vehicle, giving each of them a nod. "Good morning," he said. "I hope you don't mind me intruding? I thought you'd appreciate your driveway being clear of snow. I did the rest of town yesterday, but I didn't know that there would be people staying up here for Christmas. I'd have cleared it if I had."

"Thank you," said Sergeant Spencer. "It's appreciated. Have you heard any news about Christoph? I went to town early this morning to check on him, and the doctor was pleased with his progress."

"The nurses were changing shifts as I was heading this way," said Angus. "One of them told me pretty much the same as you just have. He's doing well. They're hoping he might wake up later today." He walked to the back of the tractor and opened a metal storage box fitted to the frame. Lifting a large cardboard box from inside, he smiled at Millie and her family. "My wife and I thought you might like some local produce."

"That's very thoughtful of you," said Millie. "Thank you."

Watching the man as he carried the box, Millie wondered once more if he might be a werewolf. He certainly moved with a fluidity that suggested he was fit and strong, but she couldn't assume that a man was capable of shifting into a fearsome beast just because he looked after himself.

She put the thought from her mind, deciding to let it float away on the cold wind that blew off the mountain. She'd never ask him, so it didn't matter what she thought.

Placing the cardboard box on the table, Angus gazed up at the huge pine tree that Millie and Judith had decorated. "How the heck did you do that?" he asked, craning his neck to look up at the star. "Those decorations are out of this world."

"We like to celebrate Christmas properly," said Judith. "We did it when we got here yesterday — with the aid of a ladder from the outhouse, and a couple of hours, it was quite easy."

"Where did you get the decorations from?" asked Angus. "They don't look real — they look as if they're part of the tree. They're fantastic!"

"We brought them with us," said Millie. "Edna told us this tree was right next to the cabin. She suggested we decorate it."

"Well," said Angus, turning his attention back to the cardboard box. "There is something good to be said about the South — it has the best Christmas decorations." He gave a broad grin and a wink. "I'm only joking, I've got nothing against you people — I'm sorry I was so rude when you arrived in the Kilted Stag yesterday. I was on the drink. My ego got the best of me. I've brought this box of supplies as an apology."

As he began removing brown paper bags from the box, Judith peered inside one of them. "Oh. My. Gosh!" she said. She reached inside and withdrew a golden finger of biscuit, sprinkled liberally with sugar. "Shortbread!"

"Home-made," said Angus, a glint in his eye. "Sophie made them. I've got a great wife there. She sent you a big hunk of her Christmas cake too, and some cookies and home-made chocolates. I've added some vegetables from my own garden — I thought they'd go well with your Christmas dinner. And there's a couple of loaves of freshly baked bread. Sophie's added cranberries to one, and olives to the other." He gave another wink. "She likes to experiment. The only thing I couldn't bring you is a turkey and some pigs-in-blankets. Assuming you're not vegetarians, of course."

"No," said Sergeant Spencer. "We're not vegetarians. Anyway, I telephoned the local butcher before we left to come here. I ordered my turkey and other meat. We'll be picking it up later today. Thank you for these things. It's a really kind gesture."

Opening another paper bag, Judith's face lit up. She gave a grin. "Fudge!"

"Don't let Sophie hear you calling it that," said Angus, his eyes alive with good humour. "It's called Tablet. It's unique to Scotland. It looks like fudge, but it's not."

Judith popped a piece into her mouth, her eyes widening as she chewed. "It's gorgeous," she mumbled. "Thank you."

"Well," said Angus. "I feel very ashamed about last night. I wasn't really going to hurt Christoph. The drink got the better of me. If he had been in his house when we got there, I wouldn't have done anything. I'm not that sort of man. I'm all drunken bark, but no bite."

"We all have our faults," said Millie.

Angus nodded. "I've been thinking about who might have attacked him, and I've got a name for you. If you're interested in investigating further, that is. A man who my wife and I think could have been responsible. He has a violent past, and he and Christoph often drink together — they argue together when they're drunk, too. It could have something to do with him. If not, I don't know who to suggest. Our town isn't really filled with hooligans."

Sergeant Spencer took the folded piece of paper that Angus handed him. He glanced at it briefly and put in his pocket. "Thank you. I'll speak to him."

Angus gave a swift nod. "I'd be quick about going to the butchers to collect your turkey if I were you. There seem to be a few problems. I've heard that orders have been mixed up and that some people aren't getting their turkeys at all. It's normally a very well-run and trustworthy business — but from what I've heard, things aren't going to plan there today."

"We'll go right away," said Sergeant Spencer.

"In fact," continued Angus. "The whole town seems a little odd today."

"Odd?" asked Millie.

"Aye, odd," said Angus. "Some people are acting

very strange. There are people, who I consider to be completely rational, insisting that they saw Santa Claus last night, flying — with the sleigh and everything. I'm of the mind that those people probably smoked a bit of the old *wacky-baccy*, if you know what I mean."

"We know," said Judith.

"Other people are insisting that there are some sort of creatures in their homes. It must be rats — an old farm building was demolished last week, and when that happens, the rats look for new homes. In this cold, they'll be looking for someplace warm. And more people have been talking about a man with a beard looking through their windows last night — *after* we found Christoph — so we know it wasn't him. Whoever it is, he's still out there. Nobody's been burgled, and nothing's been stolen, but several people have seen him."

"Okay," said Sergeant Spencer. "I can't help with rats. Or people imagining they've seen Santa Claus, but if anybody wants to speak to me about the man they've seen peering into their homes, they're more than welcome. Until the local police can get through, I don't mind standing in."

Extending a large hand, which Sergeant Spencer took without hesitation, Angus nodded. "Thank you. You'll be appreciated — by the right-thinking people in the town, anyway. There will always be some who don't trust outsiders, but pay no heed to them. They mean well."

"I'll bear that in mind," said Sergeant Spencer. "Thank you, Angus."

With a broad smile, Angus nodded at each of them in turn, and then his eyes fell on the Christmas tree once more, and a bushy eyebrow lifted. "Is that one of those little parrot things? With a robin under its wing?"

"It's just a silly Christmas decoration," said Millie, glancing at the branch on which Reuben sat rigidly, with the little robin snuggled into his feathers.

"It's very lifelike," noted Angus. "What a strange decoration. What does that have to do with Christmas?"

"I'm not sure," said Millie, grasping the tall man by his elbow and guiding him towards his tractor. "It was just one of those silly decorations you see in those cheap pound shops. I like birds, so I bought it."

"Each to their own," said Angus, climbing into the tractor cab. "Everybody's Christmas is different, and there seems to be somebody in Kilgrettin taking their Christmas really seriously this year. Somebody's building snowmen — all over the place. The outskirts of town are full of them — on the hills, in the forests. It's quite a sight — somebody's very dedicated. The kids love it — the older ones are trying to count how many they can find."

"We saw some," said Judith. "On the footpath into town."

The tractor engine started with a roar, and diesel fumes rose into the cold air. "If it snows again, I'll be back to plough the driveway for you. If you need any help, just come and ask me. I'm not hard to find."

With a crunch of gears and a growl from the powerful engine, the tractor pulled away, rocking on its high rear wheels.

When it had reached the end of the driveway and turned right, Sergeant Spencer narrowed his eyes as he looked at Millie. "You didn't fly that car again last night, did you?" he asked.

"No," said Millie. "Of course not. I promised I wouldn't."

Her father nodded. "I had to ask. You heard what Angus said, people think they saw Santa."

"The one thing they've probably all got in common," giggled Judith, "is that they probably stank of booze when they saw him. Who knows what they saw — maybe they saw a shooting star, maybe they saw nothing. It only takes one person to believe they saw something, to start a mass hallucination among susceptible people. I watched a programme about it."

"I suppose so," said Sergeant Spencer, placing greasy plates back on the tray. "Bring the box that Angus brought into the cabin, girls," he said. "Then we'll get to town and find out if the butcher has got the turkey I ordered." He lifted the tray and crunched through the snow towards the cabin. "And after that, we'll speak to the man Angus mentioned. If he attacked Christoph then we'll have found the culprit, if not, we'll let the Scottish police investigate when the snow clears."

Chapter 10

Sergeant Spencer parked the SUV outside the butcher's shop. "It's hectic in there," he said.

"It is Christmas Eve," noted Millie, gazing through the shop's large window, the glass decorated with images of reindeers and snowmen. She watched as a small crowd of people pushed and tugged at one another as they stood at the counter, behind which a flustered looking woman stood.

"Something's going on," said Sergeant Spencer.

"We might not be able to buy a turkey at this rate," said Judith. "Angus was right, there seems to be some sort of problem in there."

As they entered the shop, two women clutching shopping bags hurried out. "What a mess," said one of them.

"I know," said the other lady. "Annie is falling apart. What on earth was Clive thinking? Leaving town at his busiest time of year!"

"There's more to it than meets the eye," said the first lady. "Did you see the lines under her eyes? She didn't sleep last night. If you ask me, her and Clive have split up, and Clive has left her in the lurch!"

The women continued gossiping as they hurried along the pavement, chased by the flurries of powder snow that the biting wind whipped up.

Millie rolled her eyes, smiling at her sister. "Every town has its gossips," she said.

As they entered the shop, the interior cool and clean, a woman tugged at the hood of her son's coat as he rolled on the floor, mumbling something about his urgent requirement for chocolate. "Get up," hissed the woman, rolling her eyes in frustration at Millie and Judith. "You're embarrassing me!"

"I don't care!" shouted the boy, his little feet kicking at a display laden with bags of pork scratchings. "I want chocolate, and then I want to go home and wait for Santa!"

The lady glared into her son's face. "Santa doesn't come until tonight, when you're fast asleep in bed, Billy, and if you don't behave, he won't come at all… but you know who will come instead? You know who Santa sends to visit naughty children?"

"Snowmen," murmured Billy, a look of concern flashing across his face.

"Yes," said the mother. "And not just any snowmen! Nasty snowmen who will come and turn you into a snowman for the rest of Christmas, so all the good children can have fun without you spoiling it for them! You wouldn't like that, would you?"

"No!" said Billy, getting to his knees, his arms folded tight across his chest.

"Then get to your feet," said the mother. "We have to get home. I'm having a bad enough day today as it is, without you playing up."

"Don't care!"

"You know what will happen, Billy!" warned the mother. "You know what your brother told you — Santa's nasty snowmen will be gathering around Kilgrettin, keeping an eye out for naughty children. You'd better be good for the rest of the day, or they'll come for you!"

Contemplating what his mother had said, Billy clambered to his feet. "I'll be good, Mummy," he said, his brown eyes twinkling.

"Good," said the mother, picking up her shopping bag. "I was lucky enough to get my turkey, now I have to get home to prepare it."

As she guided her son towards the door, she winked at Millie. "If you've got kids, use that little story to keep them on their best behaviour at this time of year. My eldest son invented it last week, and it's kept Billy under control ever since!" She threw the end of her scarf over her shoulder and shrugged. "*Mostly* under control, I should say!"

With that, the mother and son left the shop, and Millie turned her attention to the small crowd jostling for position at the shop's glass counter.

Raised voices bounced off the tiled walls, and the flustered woman behind the counter appeared to be on the verge of tears as she served a particularly aggressive female customer.

"I paid a deposit in October, Annie McCluskey," said the woman with formidable eyes and a long wool coat. A felt-hat, sporting a fake flower, balanced on her perm as she bobbed her head aggressively. "You make sure I get one of those turkeys!"

"I'm trying, Edith," said Annie, flicking through the pages of a large notebook. She ran a finger down the page. "Here you are. Number twenty-nine." She turned her back on the customers and hurried through an arch, disappearing into the rear of the building. When she returned, she shook her head slowly. "I'm afraid yours was one of the ones that didn't make it, Edith."

Edith appeared to stop breathing and then closed her eyes. She took a deep breath through her nose and sighed. "I'm afraid I can't accept that, Annie. I have five people coming for dinner tomorrow. I need that turkey. I suggest you give me one of the turkeys that didn't spoil. It was your stupidity that caused the problem. You should make it right!"

"I want one, too!" said another lady. "We all do. You should give us each one of those turkeys back there. Forget those numbers in that book. We bothered to get here early. You should give the birds out on a first-come, first-served basis."

"Yes!" agreed a man. "I've been buying my

turkeys from you for twenty-five years, Annie. I paid in full for mine — not just a deposit. It's not my fault that you switched one of the fridges off. I want my turkey from the fridge that stayed on!"

"Clive normally deals with those sorts of things," said Annie. "I make the sausages and serve people. And I make the eggnog too, of course. Would anybody like some? For free — it's as good as it is every year!"

Edith stepped closer to the counter. "You make wonderful eggnog, Annie. You always have. Everybody who drinks it has always said there's something about it that makes Christmas seem more special. I don't know what that ingredient is — bourbon, I suspect, but I'm afraid your eggnog isn't going to make Christmas special for anybody who can't put a turkey on their table." She moved to the left and lifted the hatch set in the counter. She shook her head as Annie tried to stop her. "I'm coming through, Annie. I paid my deposit, and I'll pay the rest of the money I owe you, but I'm not leaving this shop without a turkey."

As Edith attempted to push past Annie, more customers rushed towards the open hatch. Three abreast, they tried to push through the narrow gap.

"Stop!" protested Annie, being pushed backwards by the small crowd. "Stop!"

"*Everybody* stop!" yelled Sergeant Spencer, using his bulk to push his way through the crowd. He pulled two people from out of the hatchway and stared at

Edith. "The shop owner doesn't want you on this side of the counter, madam. Please respect her wishes."

Edith screwed her face into a scowl and pushed her glasses along her nose. "And who the devil do you think you are?"

Retrieving his wallet from his pocket, Sergeant Spencer flashed his badge at the irate woman. "I'm a Police Officer," he said. "And I'm shocked and dismayed at the behaviour being displayed in this shop. Now, I don't know what's happened — but I do know that the way you people are acting is totally unacceptable." He looked at Annie and gave her a gentle smile. "Are you okay?"

"No," said Annie. "Everything's gone wrong. These people are right to be angry. I ruined half of the turkeys. We have two large walk-in refrigerators. Normally my husband deals with the temperatures, but he's had to… leave town. I turned one of the fridges off by accident. Had the door remain closed, the turkeys might have been okay, but unfortunately, I couldn't get that right either. It's a disaster! I don't know what to do!"

"You can give us those turkeys from the good fridge," demanded a woman, jabbing a finger towards the archway behind Annie. "Your mess up shouldn't affect my Christmas! I'm disgusted! You should be ashamed of yourself!"

Her shoulders tense, Millie tried her best to bite her tongue, but the words came, nonetheless. "I thought this was supposed to be a close-knit town," she said. "There's nothing close-knit about what's going on in here. Look at you all, attacking that poor lady. She made a mistake. Nothing is going to change that, but you could all put your heads together and come up with some sort of resolution."

Edith, apparently the ringleader, approached her. "A stranger?" she hissed. "Telling us what we should do in our town? Who do you think you are, young lady?"

Millie closed the space between herself and the bitter old lady. "Yes," she said. "I am a stranger, and judging from the behaviour of some of you, I'm happy to be a stranger. I don't think I'd like to live among people who can't look out for one another."

"What do you expect us to do?" said somebody in the crowd. "It's Christmas Day tomorrow, and half of the turkeys are ruined."

"We ordered a turkey, too," said Millie. "But if ours is ruined, so be it. If it isn't ruined, and my father and sister are in agreement, then I'll gladly share half of the meat with somebody who hasn't got one."

"I don't mind," said Judith. "I think that's a fantastic idea. There'll be plenty of meat to go around."

"That's fine by me," said Sergeant Spencer. "If we've got a turkey, we'll cook it tomorrow, carve it, and then we'll share the meat."

The room remained quiet for a few moments, and then the timid voice of a woman from the back of the crowd spoke up. "If my turkey's okay, I don't mind sharing, either."

"Or me, I don't mind helping out a neighbour," said a middle-aged lady. She smiled at Edith. "You said you had to serve five people tomorrow? Well, there's only myself and my husband eating turkey, and we always order one that's too large for us. If Annie has mine in the good fridge, you can share it — and as you're such a wonderful cook, Edith, if you'd like to roast it, then I'd be happy to come and get some of the meat when it's done."

"I — I don't know what to say," said Edith. "Thank you, Emma. That's a lovely offer."

"There," said Sergeant Spencer, his voice booming over the heads of the people in the shop. "That's better."

"We *are* a community," said a man in a bobble hat. "We should *never* forget that. We should be embarrassed about what we've done here today. Annie's obviously had some difficulties, and instead of helping her, we've attacked her." He shuffled to the counter and offered Annie his hand in apology. "I'm sorry, Annie," he said.

"Thank you, George," said Annie. "And there's no need for apologies — I understand. Now, let's concentrate on working out how to dispense the remaining turkeys. In the meantime, why doesn't everybody have a good glug of my eggnog? It will soon cheer you up! Not too much, though — Edith was correct, there is a *little* extra magic in it."

Ladling the vivid yellow liquid into small glasses, Annie handed them out with relief on her face. Then she turned to Sergeant Spencer. "Thank you," she said. She looked at Millie. "Thank you, too, what you said was lovely. It reminded us that we're a community."

"Is there anything we can do to help?" offered Sergeant Spencer, sipping eggnog. His eyes widened, and he took another sip. "Wow," he said. "That is good. I get the feeling I shouldn't be driving after drinking it."

"You'll be fine as long as you don't have any more," said Annie.

Judith licked her lips as she tasted hers, and Millie rolled a mouthful over her tongue, trying to work out what the ingredient was that made her want more and gave her a pleasant tingle in her throat. "It is good," she said, a ball of warmth in her chest.

"It's a traditional family recipe," said Annie. "I make it every year. I like to think it brings a little festive cheer to the town." She smiled up at Sergeant Spencer. "And as for your offer of help, you've done enough already." She looked away fleetingly, her eyes dropping. "My husband… left town unexpectedly. This is his business — I'm no butcher — I just do the books and make sausages. He always said it was harder than he made it look, and he was right."

"Is everything okay?" asked Millie, not wanting to intrude in the woman's personal life, but recalling what the two gossips had hinted at. "I don't want to be nosy, but the two women who left the shop earlier were gossiping, they suggested that —"

"Let me guess," said Annie, crossing her arms. "They think Clive has left me, don't they? Well, they're wrong. Clive was unexpectedly called away to… a family member, who was, erm… taken ill. With the flu! They have no business to be gossiping about me, but that's how it is in small towns like this. You can't expect your personal business to remain your own — everybody finds out soon enough."

"Anyway," she said, smiling at Sergeant Spencer. "You're obviously the gentleman that Clive told me had phoned ahead for a turkey. He said you were spending Christmas in Kilgrettin." She ran her finger down the sheet of paper in front of her. "Yours is one of the turkeys that hasn't spoiled. I'll get it for you."

As Annie scurried into the other room, Sergeant Spencer cleared his throat. "We have a turkey," he announced. "Who would like half?"

"We're all sorted," said Edith, her lips yellow with eggnog. "We've decided that those of us who have turkeys will cook them, and anybody who would like some is welcome to it. It's easier than sharing half the meat with somebody else, but thank you for the suggestion. You've been a great help." Sipping more eggnog, she stood on tiptoes and planted her lips on the policeman's cheek. "Have a wonderful Christmas!"

His cheeks blushing red, Sergeant Spencer mumbled something and smiled as Annie appeared with a plump turkey in her arms. "Here you are," she said, placing it on the counter. "One large turkey."

As Sergeant Spencer settled the bill, Annie looked at Millie and Judith from beneath thin eyebrows. "It says in the book that you're staying up at Edna Brockett's cabin?"

"That's right," said Millie.

Annie's eyes narrowed, and she lowered her voice. "You're friends of Edna's?"

"Yes," answered Judith. "She's a friend of ours."

"Have you, how do I put this — ever noticed anything… Slightly odd about the lady?" she ventured.

"Odd?" said Millie. "What you mean by odd?"

"Oh," said Annie. "I don't know, I mean — does she seem unusual to you in any way?"

"Not really," said Judith. "Why? Does she seem unusual to you?"

"No, she doesn't," said Annie, looking away quickly. "I'm being rude. I'm sorry, it's just that I haven't seen Edna for so long. I'm probably muddling her up with somebody else I thought was odd. Ignore me."

With the turkey safely in the boot of the SUV, Sergeant Spencer unfolded the piece of paper in his pocket and glanced at it. "What do you think, girls? Shall we go and ask this gentleman if he knows anything about what happened to Christoph Gruber?"

"I think we should," said Millie. "That poor man. He was lucky not to have died last night."

Turning the key in the ignition, Sergeant Spencer nodded. "Okay," he said. "We'll ask him a few questions and then go and check on Christoph — then we'll go home and enjoy our first Christmas Eve as a family."

Chapter 11

"At least the satnav works," said Sergeant Spencer, following the instructions of the polite lady, whose voice had been programmed into the little machine. "I bet they don't have internet here, though."

"I must say," said Judith, as the SUV turned onto a narrow street lined with terraced houses, most of them displaying Christmas decorations of one sort or another. "That not being able to use my mobile phone has been quite liberating. I didn't realise how addicted I'd become."

Feeling exactly the same, Millie had enjoyed not reaching for her phone every few minutes. Never one to have been completely addicted to social media sites, she had found herself using them more in recent months. It was time for a detox, and what better excuse than having no mobile phone signal?

As she was contemplating modern society's problems with technology, Sergeant Spencer slammed the brakes on and shouted. "Dammit! I could have killed her!" He pressed the horn and opened the window. "Be careful! You'll get yourself killed," he shouted at the woman, who glanced over her shoulder and continued to run along the road.

"What's wrong with her?" asked Millie.

"She ran out of that house," said Judith, pointing at a house with an open front door.

Then, a man appeared in the doorway. Wearing a Christmas jumper and a pair of tracksuit trousers, he approached the SUV and took a drag on his cigarette. "Did you see which way she went?" he asked, blowing out a cloud of smoke.

"That way," said Sergeant Spencer, pointing. "You should warn her about being more careful. I almost killed her."

The man shook his head. "I think she's going mad!" he said. "She ran out of the house saying that a little person had spoken to her. I don't know what's got into her. Never mind, she's probably gone to her mother's. That's where she goes when I annoy her — it's probably where she'll go when she imagines little people are talking to her, too."

As the man closed the door to his home, and then sauntered along the pavement, leaving a cloud of smoke in his wake, Judith frowned. "That was odd."

"That's the Scottish for you," said Reuben. "I've been here less than twenty-four hours, and already I've decided they're all as mad as a box of badgers."

Driving a little more cautiously, Sergeant Spencer made a right turn when the satnav lady politely made the suggestion.

Detached, and with extensive front gardens, the homes in the street were far larger than the terraced houses they'd just driven past.

Finding the number he was looking for, Sergeant Spencer parked the SUV and led the way up the slippery driveway.

It was at least half a minute until somebody opened the blue front door, and when she did, Millie took a step backwards. The woman looked mad. Not angry, but swivel-eyed, hair tugging mad.

She stared at the three people standing on her doorstep, unblinking, and taking deep ragged breaths.

"Hello," offered Sergeant Spencer, glancing at the sheet of paper in his hand.

Knowing her father had an excellent memory for names, Millie guessed it was an excuse to break eye contact with the scary woman with the short-cropped hair and smudged lipstick.

"We're police officers," continued her father. "I'm Sergeant Spencer, and these young ladies are Officers Thorn and Spencer. We're here to speak to a Mister Gavin Andrews. Is he here?"

"Gavin?" stammered the woman, glancing nervously over her shoulder into the house. "No. Gavin left for London last week — to start a new job." Looking over her shoulder again, her lips trembling, she ran a hand through her hair. "What do you want him for? He hasn't been in trouble for months."

"May I ask who you are?" asked Judith.

"I'm his mother," said the lady, a distant whiff of alcohol on her breath. Catherine Andrews. I'm here on my own. Gavin won't be back for Christmas."

"And he's definitely not here?" asked Millie, wondering why the woman continued to cast furtive glances into the gloom of her home.

"I told you," she said. "He's not here."

"Okay," said Sergeant Spencer. "We believe you. We're sorry to have disturbed you. Have a wonderful Christmas."

Nodding, the woman began to close the door, but then a high-pitched voice screeched from within the house. "You'd better get back here! I'm not happy with you!"

"Oh, dear," said Mrs Andrews. "Oh, dear."

"Are you okay, Mrs Andrews?" said Sergeant Spencer. "Is everything all right?"

The woman's knees buckled, and Sergeant Spencer reached for her, catching her beneath her arms. He lifted her to her feet, steadying her. "Let's get you inside," he said, gently leading her along the hallway.

"He's so angry, and he won't stop judging me!" wailed Mrs Andrews. "Since yesterday. He went somewhere last night after I saw a man looking in through the window, and when he got back this morning, he was even angrier!"

Millie cast a glance in Judith's direction, which her sister reciprocated.

Mrs Andrews must have been talking about her son. When Mrs Andrews had told her son she'd seen a man with a white beard looking through the window, he must've jumped to the same conclusion that Angus had when his children had seen the man. He'd assumed it had been Christoph Gruber.

"Do you have any idea where he went last night?" asked Sergeant Spencer, his raised eyebrow telling Millie that he'd reached the same conclusion as she had.

"No," said Mrs Andrews, trembling. "But thank goodness you've come. I haven't slept all night. I've been terrified. I've never been so scared. Will you make him go away?"

"It's awful that you're so afraid of your own son, Mrs Andrews," said Judith. "But if he's done what we think he's done; he'll probably be going away for quite some time."

"My son?" said Mrs Andrews, confusion on her face. "Oh, my son — he's in London."

"Get in here!" came the angry voice from the room at the end of the hallway. "I told you. You'd better be good today!"

"Oh, my goodness," said Mrs Andrews. "I've tried to be good since yesterday, but nothing is good enough for *him*."

"Mrs Andrews," asked Millie, a deep discomfort

growing within her. "Who is that doing the shouting? Is that Gavin?"

"Gavin is in London," mumbled Mrs Andrews. "Please make him leave my house. He won't go away."

Releasing Mrs Andrews from his gentle grasp, Sergeant Spencer stroked his chin as he looked at Millie and Judith. "Something's not right," he said.

"Well deduced, Sherlock," said Reuben, from within Millie's pocket.

Mrs Andrews spun on the spot. "Who said that? Is it another one? I heard a little voice coming from behind me!"

"It was me," said Millie, startled, giving her pocket a gentle warning tap with her open hand. "I've got a bit of a frog in my throat."

"You'd better hurry!" came the voice from the end of the hallway. "What are you doing? Are you being naughty?"

Mrs Andrews stared at Millie, horror in her eyes. "Help me," she mouthed, her words a rasping whisper.

Millie nodded and hurried along the hallway. Fully expecting to see Gavin Andrews sprawled on the sofa when she entered the room, she looked around in puzzlement. There was nobody there. With ornaments and newspapers strewn across the floor, and a Christmas tree laying on its side, its baubles and decorations scattered across the carpet, the room was a mess.

Having expected the room to have been tidier, judging by the neatness of the front garden and the hallway through which they'd entered, Millie looks around once more, as a breeze blowing through the open window flicked newspaper pages open. "Hello?" she said, checking behind the sofa. "Is there somebody here?"

"Gavin Andrews?" asked Sergeant Spencer.

"He must have got out through here," said Judith, leaning through the open window. "I don't see anybody, though."

"What's been happening, Mrs Andrews?" asked Millie, taking the frightened woman's shaking hand. "Who was here? Was it Gavin? What's he been doing to you? Did he make this mess?"

"Gavin is in London," stammered Mrs Andrews. She lifted an arm which shook like a tree in the wind and pointed at the row of three shelves screwed to the wall above the fireplace. "It was him," she half-whispered. "Please take him away. I don't like him."

"Who?" asked Millie.

Mrs Andrews pointed again, this time taking a step closer to the shelves. "Him!" she spat.

"The Christmas decoration?" asked Millie, staring at the little ornament.

"It's not a decoration," said Mrs Andrews. "It's alive. I've never seen it before, until yesterday."

"It's one of those elves on a shelf," noted Judith.

"A what, on a what?" said Sergeant Spencer.

"They're all the rage," explained Judith.

"They're to make children good at Christmas time. Parents tell them that the elf has been sent by Santa and that he watches them all day, and then magically travels back to Santa at night-time — to tell him if the kids have been naughty or nice. Parents move them around the house, pretending they're moving on their own."

"Oh," said Sergeant Spencer. "I suppose that could be fun." He looked away from the colourful toy elf, sitting on the top shelf, its legs dangling beneath it. "Mrs Andrews, are you all right? I'm a little concerned about you."

Millie indicated the open whiskey bottle with an almost imperceptible jerk of the head.

Her father nodded. "Have you had a little drink?" he asked.

"You would, too," whispered Mrs Andrews. She pointed at the elf. "You would, too. If that was watching you."

"It's just a toy," said Sergeant Spencer. "You must have put it there when you put up the Christmas decorations."

"I've never seen it before," said Mrs Andrews, her bottom lip wobbling. "It's not a decoration. It's a creature. An evil little creature."

"Mrs Andrews," said Sergeant Spencer, approaching the shelf and reaching for the elf. "It's not a creature, it's a —"

Judith's scream made Sergeant Spencer jump. He stumbled backwards. Then, he looked up at the shelf and gave his own throaty warble. "What in the name of—"

The little elf, no taller than a mobile phone, and now quite obviously alive, hopped in anger from foot to foot. Its narrow face angry, and its tiny hands balled into fists, it screamed at Sergeant Spencer. "Don't try and touch me, fat lad," it squealed, its little teeth bared. "You're not allowed to touch me. My magic will leave me if you touch me, and then how will I know if she's been naughty or nice?"

"That's what they tell the kids," said Judith, backing away towards the open door. "They tell them not to touch them because they'll lose their magic, and Santa will be angry."

"The child is correct!" shouted the elf, scurrying from left to right along the shelf, the little green hat it wore over its bright red hair swinging as it moved. "Santa will be angry if you touch me, and Catherine won't get any presents tonight when he visits!"

"I don't want any presents," said Mrs Andrews, pouring herself a whiskey, the bottle clanking against the glass as her hand shook. "I just want this nightmare to end."

"I'm taking note of that as well, Catherine," said the elf. A large piece of yellowed paper appeared in one hand, and a little fountain pen in the other. He licked the nib before putting it to the paper. "A fifth drink of naughty juice before midday," he said as he wrote.

The paper vanished, and he placed the pen

behind his pointed ear. "Santa will not be happy with you, Catherine. You wait until I tell him what you've been up to. Drinking alcohol! Not going to sleep at the proper time. Swearing. Calling me names. Drinking from the milk carton. Trying to hit me with a Christmas tree. Trying to set fire to me with a deodorant can and a lighter. If you're expecting presents tonight, Catherine, I have a feeling you're going to be awfully disappointed."

Catherine slumped onto the sofa and downed the glass of whiskey in one long swallow. She gave a cough and then stared at the elf. "You've made a mess of my living room, you've made me think I'm insane, and you keep judging me! Please go! Please leave me alone!"

"Ha," said the elf, the paper appearing in his hand again. "Another bullet point for the naughty note. Telling lies!" The paper vanished again, and he scowled in Catherine's direction. "I didn't make this mess. You made the mess in this room — when you were chasing me around!"

Suddenly, and with great speed for such a bulky man, Sergeant Spencer pushed himself forward on the balls of his feet, his arm outstretched as he attempted to grab the mysterious creature.

With astonishing speed, far quicker than the policeman's, the elf leapt from the shelf and landed on the messy coffee table. It stood with its little legs wide apart, and its thumbs on its pointed ears. It wiggled its fingers, and a tiny pink tongue waggled between its lips. "You can't catch me!" it teased. "I'm far too fast for you!"

Sergeant Spencer stared at Millie, horror on his face. "The woman I almost ran over must have seen one of these, and Angus did say people were reporting strange things. Do you think this has got anything to do with that stray bolt of magical energy you and Judith sent flying into town last night?"

Millie stared at the elf and then swallowed. Had she and Judith somehow opened a gate to The Chaos? The other dimension in which evil creatures lived. The dimension from which Reuben himself had come. The awful place Millie had visited to save her father from losing all of his memories.

She hoped not. It wasn't possible. *Was it?*

Since Millie's visit to The Chaos, the magical community, with the help of two non-paranormal scientists, had worked tirelessly to find an answer. After a lot of hard work, they'd found a way to lock the gate. Nothing had passed through it for months.

Had the magic she and Judith had accidentally emitted last night caused a rift between the two dimensions? Surely not — because if it had, not only had she and Judith caused a lot of problems in Kilgrettin — they'd also be in a lot of trouble when Henry Pinkerton found out.

"Where did you come from?" asked Millie, staring at the little elf. "From another dimension?"

"I just exist," said the elf. "I didn't come from anywhere. I'm just me!"

Feeling a rustling in her pocket, Millie looked down to see Reuben clambering from her coat. He stared at the elf. "He's not from The Chaos! There's no creature like that in The Chaos. He wouldn't last two seconds in that hell-hole!"

The sound of clinking glass reverberated through the room and Mrs Andrews drank another generous shot of whiskey, her horrified eyes on Millie's pocket. "What now?" she said. "What now?"

"A fine beast!" said the elf, studying Reuben. "What manner of creature is it?"

Launching himself from Millie's pocket, with a loud flapping of wings and a squawk, Reuben thrust himself in the direction of the elf.

The tiny creature bounded across the table, and launched itself towards the curtain rail, seemingly defying physics as it sailed through the air.

"These humans might not be quick enough to catch you," squawked Reuben, changing direction in mid-flight. "But I certainly am! Come here, you little shit!"

The elf emitted a cackling laugh, and ran along the curtain rail, glancing over its shoulder as Reuben neared it. As Reuben made a sweeping left turn, his beak open as he closed in on the little creature, the elf leapt into the air, and with remarkable dexterity, swung itself into position on the cockatiel's back.

With the little man grabbing the feathers on his cheeks, Reuben squawked in horror. "Get off me!" he yelled. He looked at Millie in panic. "Get it off me! I don't like it! I want to go home now!"

Not caring that Mrs Andrews might see, and not caring what her father or Henry Pinkerton might think, Millie drew on her magic. With the spell poised at her fingertips, she aimed at the cockatiel with the little elf on its back.

Hunched like a jockey on a racehorse, the elf flew Reuben in circles around the room, and just before she cast the spell, Millie stopped herself.

Her spells had gone awry before, and she did not want to hurt her familiar. Instead, she attempted to negotiate with the magical creature on his back. "Why don't you come down here?" she suggested. "Perhaps we could all be friends?"

"No chance!" screeched the elf, tugging a fistful of feathers on the side of Reuben's face, forcing him to turn. "I'm going to go and tell Santa how naughty Catherine's been. I'm going to ride this beast there. Santa's not expecting me until it gets dark, but when I tell him just how naughty Catherine's been, he'll understand. He might even make me Top Elf! And that means that I can come with him tonight when he delivers the presents!"

Then, as the elf dug his heels into Reuben's flanks, making the little bird squawk, Millie understood what it intended to do. Twisting the feathers on Reuben's face, the little man forced the bird to fly towards the open window. Before Millie could even think about casting a spell, the elf had ridden Reuben through the window and into the sunshine.

Leaning from the window, Millie stared upwards as Reuben gained altitude, the little elf still laughing as it rode her familiar into the sun. "Don't worry, Reuben!" she shouted. "We'll find you!"

Then, drifting on the breeze, came Reuben's screeching voice. "I hate Scotland!" he squawked. "I really hate Scotland!"

Chapter 12

With Mrs Andrews still slumped on the sofa, slurping neat whiskey from the bottle, Millie looked at her sister and father in shock. "Reuben's just been stolen by an elf," she said. "What is going on?"

"It must be the magic that you two sent flying towards Kilgrettin last night," said Sergeant Spencer. "It has to be!"

"I hate to admit it," said Judith, staring through the window at the empty sky. "But I concur. There's no other explanation."

The connection with her familiar like an invisible thread of energy, Millie sensed he was okay. If anything happened to Reuben, she'd feel it in her very soul, like an identical twin might know when their sibling has been injured. Anyway, Reuben lived a charmed life. He was protected by magic, and he possessed a cunning streak a mile wide. He'd be okay. *She hoped.*

"You saw it!" said Mrs Andrews. "You saw it, didn't you?" She got to her feet, and hurried across the room, slamming the window shut and shaking a fist at the sky. "And don't come back, you wee bawbag!"

"Mrs Andrews," said Sergeant Spencer, his face devoid of colour. "We're going to have to leave — are you going to be all right on your own?"

Mrs Andrews remained at the window, staring skyward. "I'll be fine," she promised. "I'm going to get Gavin's old air rifle from the shed, and if that colourful wee bastard returns, I'll pop a cap right between his eyes!"

"Mrs Andrews," said Sergeant Spencer. "I don't think that's a good idea. Did you know it's illegal to discharge an air rifle in a public place?"

"And you might hit my cockatiel!" said Millie.

"Don't worry," said Mrs Andrews. "I'll only shoot at it if it comes into my home again, and I promise I won't hurt that wee bird — brave bugger that it is. After what I've been through over the last twenty-four hours, I don't even care why the bird was talking, and I don't want to know — all I know is that it deserves a medal. Now, judging from the way you've been talking about magic spells, and the fact that you have a talking bird, I have a feeling that you three people will be needed elsewhere. I'm sure I'm not the only person who'll need your help today. Something odd is happening in Kilgrettin."

As Sergeant Spencer drove towards Kilgrettin town centre, Mrs Andrews' words turned out to be prophetic. Before they'd even got to the end of the street she lived on, a young couple sprinted across the road, looking over their shoulders in horror at their home.

Judith pointed at the upstairs window of the house. "Look!" she said.

Millie stared in astonishment at the elf in the window. Larger than the one which had ridden her familiar away, it pressed its face against the glass, its mouth a wide o-shape.

It watched the young couple intently as they ran away. When they turned to look at their home once more, it indicated its eyes with two fingers, and then jabbed the same two digits at the couple. The internationally understood gesture of, *I'll be watching you*!

Scanning the sky once more for Reuben, Millie looked at her sister. "It has to be something to do with the magic we generated last night. I think we should try and find out where it landed."

Sergeant Spencer nodded, taking a left, heading towards the town centre, the car wheels losing grip on the snow as he took the corner too fast. "I think it landed on the outskirts of town. Somewhere at the base of the mountain."

Under a fresh blanket of snow, Kilgrettin shimmered and sparkled, and the town centre appeared to be normal. The Kilted Stag's little garden teemed with people dressed against the cold, smoking, drinking and talking.

Three children threw snowballs at each other, gathering snow in mittened hands from the base of the market square Christmas tree, which twinkled with colourful lights.

With not a single elf in sight, everybody seemed to be continuing life as usual. As Sergeant Spencer slowed to let a man cross the road, Judith pointed towards the pub. "It's Maggie! The pub landlady. I think she wants to speak to us."

Running as quickly as the slippery road allowed her, Maggie waved an arm, her red hair vivid in the winter landscape as she approached the vehicle.

She lowered her head as Sergeant Spencer wound down his window. She stared inside at the occupants. "I want to ask you a question," she said. "And I'd like an honest answer."

"Go on," said Millie, from the passenger seat.

Maggie narrowed her eyes and looked between the three of them as she spoke. "I know Edna Brockett very well. I know her so well, in fact, that we have something in common. Something in common that I couldn't possibly divulge to most of the people in this town. I have a feeling that you three may know what I'm talking about. If you do — now is the time to say so, because the problems the town is currently experiencing all seemed to begin when you arrived yesterday."

She licked her chapped lips. "I think you'd all agree that even though it's Christmas, there's a little bit more magic in the air than normal." She narrowed her eyes. "Do you know what I'm talking about?"

"Erm," said Judith, flashing Millie a glance. "I'm not sure what you mean."

Rolling her eyes, Maggie gave a loud sigh. "It's too cold for this. I can't be speaking in riddles — something is happening in this town, and I think it's people such as *us* who are going to get to the bottom of it."

"What do you mean?" said Sergeant Spencer, looking uncomfortable.

Tutting, Maggie thrust her hand inside the car, and without warning, expelled a flurry of bright sparks from the tips of her fingers. As the sparks drifted towards Sergeant Spencer's lap, she looked around with a smile. "Now do you know what I'm talking about?" she said.

"You're a witch," said Millie.

"And I'm guessing that you three are paranormal," suggested Maggie, allowing the sparks to cease. "Angus came to see me this morning — he told me that you've got some extraordinary Christmas tree decorations up at Edna Brockett's cabin. He told me that there is no way on earth that those decorations weren't created by magic."

"Angus?" said Millie, realising her hunch about the big man had been correct. "He knows about magic?"

"Let's just say Angus likes a full moon," hinted Maggie.

"A werewolf," said Millie.

Maggie smiled. "Yes. There's only a handful of us paranormal folk in town. We keep a very low profile. Now, if you'd like to tell me exactly who you three are, perhaps we can get to the bottom of what's going on around here. I'm hearing reports of all sorts of odd things happening in town."

"Okay," said Millie. "My sister and I are witches. Our father is non-paranormal. We think a rogue ball of magic we created last night may be causing the problems. We launched it by accident, and it landed somewhere on the outskirts of town at the foot of the mountain. We're on our way to look for it."

"We've seen some strange things, too," added Judith.

Millie nodded her agreement. "We've just come from a house where an elf has been terrorising a woman. Then the elf rode off on my familiar. He's okay, though. I can feel him." She put a finger to her forehead. "In here."

"You have a familiar?" said Maggie, tilting her head enquiringly. "It's not every witch who can keep a familiar. You must be from a strong bloodline?"

"Apparently so," said Millie. "I'm from the bloodline tasked with keeping the gate to The Chaos closed."

"The Chaos Gate in Spellbinder Bay?" asked Maggie.

Millie nodded.

"But doesn't the witch tasked with such an important task have to stay within the boundaries of Spellbinder Bay — if the gate is to remain closed?" asked Maggie. "That's what Edna always told me."

"That used to be the case," said Millie. "But we've worked out how to lock the gate. It poses no great danger anymore."

"Let's hope so," said Maggie. "Edna's told me some horror stories about that gate and the awful things that came through it."

"Maggie!" came a man's voice.

A large man hurried towards the car, a black hat on his head and his beard enveloped in a cloud of condensed breath.

"Hello, Angus," said Maggie. She gave him a smile. "It's out in the open. They know you're a werewolf — the two girls are witches and the father is a non-paranormal who knows of our community. You can speak freely."

A broad smile beneath his beard, Angus nodded. "I knew it!" he said, peering into the vehicle. "There's no way those decorations on that tree of yours were bought from a shop. I knew they were magic the moment I saw them."

"And I saw you sniffing the air at Christoph's home last night. You smelled him out, didn't you?" said Millie.

"I did indeed," said Angus. "The scent of human blood was in the air. I didn't notice it when we first arrived. The wind was against me."

"You kept that quiet, Millie," said Judith.

"I wasn't certain," said Millie. "I'm sorry."

Angus peered into the car. "And that decoration on the tree — that parrot thing and the robin? That wasn't made of plastic, was it? I saw the parrot move."

"The *cockatiel* is my familiar," said Millie. "I don't know what to say about the robin — they bonded over a plate of bacon."

Angus gave a grunting laugh. "As much as I'd like to talk about bacon, there are more important things to discuss. Let's start with Gavin Andrews. Have you spoken to him?"

"Yes," said Sergeant Spencer. "The visit didn't go without a few problems, but Gavin's not in town. It couldn't have been him who attacked Christoph."

"Well," said Angus, his voice gravelly. "That makes what I'm about to tell you even more relevant. I think I know who beat Christoph almost to death."

"Who?" said Sergeant Spencer.

"Have you been to the butcher's shop?" asked Angus.

"Yes," said Sergeant Spencer. "We were there earlier."

Angus nodded. "Are you aware that Clive has left town all of a sudden — during the busiest period of the year for his business?"

"Yes," said Judith. "We know."

"What you might not know is that Clive was seen arguing with Christoph yesterday," explained Angus. "My wife's friend was in the butcher's shop, and Christoph was in there, too. He'd been drinking. He didn't have enough money to pay for his sausages, so he asked Annie for credit. Christoph isn't the sort of man any business person in their right mind would give credit to, so when Annie refused, he didn't take the news well.

"He called Annie some awful names and threatened her. What he didn't know was that Clive was right there — in the back room. He came out wielding a stake tenderising hammer and threatened Christoph. He threw him out and told him that he'd regret speaking to his wife like that."

"And then," said Millie. "Christoph was badly beaten last night, and Clive has left town."

"Aye," said Angus. "I like Clive, but if it was him that did that to Christoph, he deserves to be punished."

"I agree," said Sergeant Spencer. "But it seems we've got more pressing issues to deal with at the moment. There seems to be some sort of magic working its way through Kilgrettin."

"Don't I know it," huffed Angus. "We've got a

bloody elf in our house — watching the kids. My kids are taking it well — but they're from the paranormal community. It doesn't scare them. In fact, they've been on their best behaviour, and the elf is polite as long as the kids are being good. People from the non-paranormal community who've seen the elves are terrified, though. They've never seen anything like it before."

"It's not just elves," said Maggie. "I saw Santa last night. And I'm not the only one. He was riding around up there, complete with his sleigh and reindeer."

Millie looked at the floor. "I don't think you saw Santa," she said. "We lied when we said we'd driven through the snow to get here yesterday. I put a spell on this car. I made it fly. It glowed, too — bright red. It was us you saw."

Maggie smiled and shook her head. "No," she said. "I know what I saw. I saw a sleigh being pulled through the sky by reindeers. Santa was at the reins. There was no mistaking him — the white beard and red coat. I saw him after I locked the pub at midnight."

"That wasn't us," said Millie. "We weren't flying around at that time."

"Then we need to get to the bottom of this," said Maggie. "The people of Kilgrettin are quite open-minded folk, but I'm not sure that they're quite ready for Santa Claus or elves just yet."

"It has to be the magic we released last night that's

causing the problems," said Millie. "We have to find out where it landed and put a stop to it."

"Magic?" asked Angus. "What magic?"

Millie explained to Angus what she'd already told Maggie. When she'd finished speaking, Angus opened the back door of the car and climbed in alongside Judith. "I'm coming with you," he said. "My senses are superior. I might see or hear something that none of you can."

"I'll get back to the pub," said Maggie, glancing over the road towards the Kilted Stag. "I opened early today because for some reason — when grown adults see a live elf on a shelf in their homes, the first place they think to go to is the pub." She smiled at Sergeant Spencer. "I'm sure you won't be chastising me for opening early and breaking the licensing laws?"

"I'm hoping you're still going to be open when we've dealt with the magic," smiled the policeman. "I think mine's going to be a large whiskey. Then one more, and then another."

Chapter 13

Having taken the SUV as far as he could along a snowy logging track, Sergeant Spencer parked alongside a stack of felled trees.

As the group trudged single file into the woodland, following a narrow path, Judith pointed into the trees. “More snowmen,” she said. “Somebody’s been busy.”

Her thighs burning as the path steepened, Millie stepped gratefully in the footprints left by her father and Angus, thankful that she didn’t need to plough a route through the snow.

Her eyes and ears open for any sign of rogue magic, she wondered how many other people had spent their twenty-sixth birthday in the way she was spending hers. Not many, she imagined.

She looked at the sky through the pine canopy, searching for Reuben. Concentrating, she summoned the bird with a thought she broadcast across the mountain, knowing he couldn't ignore her if he received it. She'd give him time to respond, but she knew he was alive and well. She could feel him.

Then, as Angus paused next to a fallen tree, sniffing the air and listening to the breeze, hoping for any sign of magic, she thought of her mother.

She'd been used to her being dead, and when she'd appeared as a ghost in Spellbinder Bay, she'd become accustomed to her mother visiting her from the other side. She hadn't visited for a while, though, and Millie knew she couldn't bring herself into existence all the way up there, in Scotland, many miles from the magical energy of Spellbinder Bay.

She followed as Angus began moving again, heading further up the mountainside, happy that she had one of her parents with her on her birthday. Pressing a hand against her coat, she smiled as she felt the shape of the pendant beneath her gloved fingers.

She watched her father as he trudged through the snow in front of her, his hot breath leaving him in clouds and his woolly hat speckled with snow.

She wondered what it would have been like to have grown up with him as her father. She imagined it would have been wonderful, but as neither she or her father had been aware of each other's existence, there had never been any chance of it becoming a reality.

Angus stopped walking again. Then he cocked his head like a dog and listened intently, his eyes closed as he concentrated. When he opened them, he shook his head. "I don't hear anything unusual," he said. "And nothing smells out of the ordinary."

"Let's keep looking," said Millie. "I have a feeling that I won't find Reuben until whatever magic is infecting the town has been dealt with."

Knocking snow from branches as they pushed through the forest, the four of them continued in single file, looking for anything that might give them a clue as to where the magic had landed.

Recalling the mushroom cloud they'd seen from the cabin when the ball of magic had dropped from the sky, Millie knew they were in the right area, but that didn't make the task of finding it any simpler. It was a vast area.

At one point, Sergeant Spencer used a hand to shield his eyes from the sun, and stared up the mountain, pointing through a gap in the trees. "That's where the cabin is," he said. "The magic must have come down around here somewhere."

They continued searching, not sure what they were looking for. Angus paused regularly to sniff the air, and to listen, but after an hour of crunching through snow crystals and checking ravines for some sort of sign, he gave a frustrated sigh. "I'm not sure we're going to find anything," he announced, his accent even broader as he powered his way up the slope, his breath swirling around his head.

"The magic can't last forever," said Judith. "It should wear out soon, of its own accord. Perhaps it already has. Perhaps there's nothing to find, and when we get back to town, everything will be back to normal."

"Time is not on our side, either," said Sergeant Spencer. "It's already mid-afternoon. It will be dark by half-past-four. Maybe we should turn back."

Knowing both her sister and father were right, but with a small voice in her head telling her to press on, Millie pushed up the slope as the others watched her progress. "If I can't see anything over the peak of the next ridge, I'll admit defeat," she croaked, forcing her thighs to propel her through the deep snow.

A golden eagle soared high above her, gliding in lazy circles as it searched for a meal. Wondering whether golden eagles ate elves or cockatiels, she crested the ridge and paused for breath. There was nothing out of the ordinary. Just more trees and snow.

She looked at the sky again, watching the eagle gliding effortlessly through the thin air. "I'll find you, Reuben," she promised.

As she dropped her eyes from the sky, she stumbled backwards, tripping in the snow, a cry of fear leaving her cold lips.

Landing with a soft thump, dread gripping her insides, she stared at the apparition.

As if struggling to make itself seen, the ghostly spectre shimmered and flickered, visible in one moment but not the next, like a fish in deep water showing its flanks to the angler who'd hooked it.

Then, clearer than the image the apparition

presented, a voice floated across the snow. The soft tones and the warmth in which the words were spoken flushed the dread from Millie's bones, and she scrambled to her feet as the voice spoke again. "It's me, Millie."

"Mum!" said Millie, reaching for the flickering form, her hand passing through it. "I can't see you."

"Too weak," came her mother's voice. "Not enough energy."

Then, as if her mother had channelled every electron of energy into one portion of her form, a single arm and hand appeared.

Constructed from gossamer-thin strands of silver energy, the hand extended a single elegant finger, the neat nail pointing up the hill.

"The magic you're looking for," said her mother. "It's why I'm able to appear. It's weak. I can't get through. Only my voice. The magic is behind you, darling. Just a short distance up the hill."

"Thank you, Mum," said Millie, reaching for the hand that floated in the frigid air.

Shifting like smoke, the hand moved towards Millie's face. As the fingers brushed her cheek, warm tingles running through her, a face formed before hers.

The eyes as warm and kind as ever, Millie stared into the beautiful face of her mother.

Then her mother's voice came again, soft and gentle. "Happy birthday, my darling."

Then she was gone, and Millie put a hand to her

cheek, tingles still dancing over her skin. She smiled, her heart warm, as if she'd sipped a whiskey.

It had been worth waiting twenty-six years for a birthday on which she'd seen both of her parents.

She wondered if she should tell her father and sister that her mother had visited, but decided against it. It had been a present she would keep to herself. She didn't want to hurt her father and Judith's feelings by telling them that the visit had made her birthday perfect, she wanted them to think it had been perfect with just the three of them and Reuben.

Scrambling up the next steep incline, Millie grabbed at thin pine branches to help her crest the peak. She studied the clearing she'd found herself in, brushing snow from her clothes.

The trees were fewer, and the view over the valley spectacular, and as she sucked in long gulps of cold air, her heart still recovering from the climb, she saw it.

It had only been a flash of colour in the corner of her eye, but when she turned to face it, she hurried towards the hollow carved into the mountainside.

Reaching the dip in the ground, the trees growing from it devoid of snow, she had no doubt that she'd discovered the magic she and her sister had generated.

The flash of colour she'd seen against the white backdrop had been a vibrant clump of daffodils, and they weren't the only flowers that had bloomed unseasonably early.

As she noticed a growth of crocus plants at the base of a pine tree, she called out, her voice echoing as it bounced off the snow-free rock and soil in the hollow. "Here! I think I've found the impact zone!"

Angus reached her first, with Judith and Sergeant Spencer in his wake. When he saw what Millie had found, he nodded. "Yes," he said. "Unless there's some weird microclimate up here, there's definitely something unusual going on."

As Millie stepped into the hollow, she silently named some of the flowers. A carpet of bluebells glowed in the winter sun, and snowdrops peeped from between the vivid heathers that created a soft carpet beneath her feet.

In a small hollow, no bigger than Edna Brockett's log cabin, winter had vanished, and a vibrant spring had taken its place.

Not a single flake of snow fell or lay on the ground, and a rabbit raised its head in alarm at the sound of approaching footsteps. Having being taking full advantage of the lush green grass which grew at the periphery of the circle, it sniffed the air before hopping into the snowy wilderness. Back into winter.

"Spring has come early to this little part of Scotland," noted Angus.

"Yes," said Millie. She pointed towards a particularly healthy patch of daffodils, their petals glowing unnaturally gold. The stalks which held up the golden crowns appearing to vibrate as if pure energy were coursing through them.

Getting to her knees, the earth warm beneath her, Millie removed her gloves and parted the daffodils, her fingers tingling as she touched the plants.

At the base of the flowers, where earth should have been, was an orb. The basketball-sized sphere emitted a soft humming sound as it glowed with bright reds, deep greens, and spectacular silvers and golds.

"Christmas colours," said Judith, kneeling next to Millie. "When we were decorating the tree, we were thinking about Christmas, and when we accidentally discharged the orb, we must have filled it with Christmas thoughts and colours. Energy must be seeping out of it and trickling through town. We must have conjured up some pretty powerful magic between us, little sister."

"Yes," said Millie, running her hand across the warm surface of the energised ball. "We did."

"But why has it turned this area into spring?" asked Angus. "If it's Christmas magic?"

"It's just heated the earth and the air in this area," said Millie, placing her hand on the ground, her palm warming immediately. "The magic has increased the speed with which the plants grow, and given them an extra helping of beauty."

"Whatever it's doing to nature," said Sergeant Spencer, removing his hat as he stepped into the warmth of the circle. "It needs to come to an end. I don't think it's any stretch of the imagination to say that this ball of magic is responsible for the sightings of Santa Claus and the elves on the bloody shelves."

"We formed it together, Judith," said Millie. "We'll have to end it together."

Removing her gloves and placing her hand on the orb alongside her sister's, their little fingers touching, Judith nodded. "Ready?"

Millie responded with a crackle of sparks at her fingertips. She smiled at her sister. "I'm ready," she confirmed. "Imagine the lights in the orb dimming and dying when you release your magic. I'll do the same."

As both witches conveyed their thoughts through the magic which left their bodies, the orb stopped humming and began making a crackling sound. Millie immediately pictured the orb fading, its lights no longer bright colours — but washed-out colours. Colours fading into nothingness.

With the two witch's magic mingling, the orb responded quickly. At first, it glowed more brightly as it crackled, as if fighting the force which was trying to snuff out its energy, but then it succumbed to the power of the very magic which had formed it.

Slowly, and with a final bright burst of Christmas colours, it ceased to glow and then ceased to exist entirely. Crumbling into dust, the orb joined the soil around it, and as soon as it had, the plants began wilting and the air became chillier.

Slipping her gloves back on, Millie let out a relieved sigh. Closing her eyes, she concentrated on her familiar, summoning him to her side. Now the magic had been dealt with, the elf that had stolen her familiar would vanish, and Reuben could come back to her.

She felt him, but she didn't sense him approaching. She'd give him time, she thought. Who knows how far that awful little elf had ridden him. They might not even be in Scotland anymore.

"I've summoned Reuben," she said to Judith. "I can sense him. Let's hope he responds."

"He will," said Judith. "Give him time. We stopped the spell. Those elves have gone."

"We'll know for sure when we get back to town," said Sergeant Spencer.

As the small group retraced their footsteps, Millie peered through the canopy whenever she got the chance, searching the darkening skies for her friend.

The golden eagle had moved on, and Reuben was nowhere to be seen. He was alive, though. She could feel him.

With her eyes still fixed on the sky, she didn't notice Judith had stopped abruptly in front of her, and she grunted as she slammed into her sister's back. "Ow! I'm sorry. I didn't know you'd stopped."

Realising that everybody else was looking at something, Millie peered around her sister. Angus stared at the object in the path, a puzzled look on his face. "It's right where our footprints are," he said. "It wasn't there when we came this way, was it? I would have seen it. We would have walked right through it."

Brushing past her sister, Millie stared at the snowman. With eyes and a mouth formed from pebbles, and the stub of a carrot for a nose, there was something about it which unnerved her.

It wasn't the snowman that perplexed her so much, but the question of who had built it. "There are no other tracks apart from ours," she said, scanning the surrounding snow. "Somebody must have followed in our footsteps."

"And those?" said Sergeant Spencer, looking into the forest.

Following her father's gaze, Millie failed to see them at first, but then her eyes found the shapes. Snowmen, and lots of them.

Everywhere she looked, there was a snowman. Some taller than others, and some plumper — they all had one thing in common; the grinning mouth and narrow eyes made from pebbles.

Unlike the snowmen she'd made as a child, with smiling faces, these snowmen looked evil. She wondered if evil was an adjective one could use to describe a snowman. She didn't care whether it was, or not. It was the word that popped into her mind, and it seemed right.

"Do you remember what that woman in the butcher's shop told her son?" said Judith, looking at Millie, her eyes wide and staring.

Millie did, and the unnerving thought had crossed her mind, too. "Yes."

"What did she tell her son?" asked Angus, sniffing the air.

Millie kept her eyes on the snowman built on the path as if it would move if she looked away. "She told him that if he wasn't good, Santa would send evil snowmen to turn him and all the naughty children into snowmen. She told him that the snowmen would be already gathering around town, waiting for tonight."

"The little boy's big brother invented the story," added Judith.

"But the little boy believed it!" said Millie. "That's what our magic did! It made things that people believe in come to life. And even though that story was only told in one family, the fact that one little boy believed in it means that it came true for everybody else, too. That's what these snowmen are. The beliefs of a little boy brought to life by our magic."

"The same applies to the elves," said Judith. "And the sightings of Santa! Lots of kids believe in them!"

"Then it's a good job we found that orb," said Sergeant Spencer. "Imagine what could have happened tonight — if you think an elf on a shelf is bad, imagine an army of evil snowmen coming for naughty children. It would have been the thing of nightmares."

"Come on," said Judith, staring at the snowmen lurking in the shadows beneath the trees. "They give me the creeps. Let's get back to town." She gave Millie a gentle smile. "And then we'll find Reuben."

Chapter 14

Everything appeared to be normal in Kilgrettin. Nobody ran screaming through the streets, and not a single elf was to be seen at a house window.

Relief flooded Millie. It was her birthday, after all, and she hadn't been enjoying feeling responsible for releasing an uncontrolled spell into the little Highland town.

She was aware that they'd got away lightly. The magic had been quite tame in reality. A few people had seen a real-life elf on their shelf, and a handful of people had seen Santa. There were far worse things that could have happened.

She closed her eyes and summoned Reuben once more. She wanted him with her on her birthday, and she peered through the car window, desperate to spot the little bird.

Angus stepped out of the SUV as Sergeant

Spencer parked in the market square. He looked into the back seat. "Don't you two girls think about casting any more spells," he chuckled. "Although I must say, it's nice to have some more paranormal people in town — even if it's just for Christmas. If you need anything else while you're here, don't hesitate to ask." As he began crunching through the snow towards the Kilted Stag, he paused. "What are you going to do about Clive, the butcher? It seems to me like he's responsible for what happened to Christoph."

"Clive's left town," said Sergeant Spencer. "There's not a lot I can do, apart from leaving it to the Scottish Police. They'll deal with it when the snow clears. I'm going to visit the Medical Centre to see how Christoph is, and when he's able to speak, we'll find out from him if it was Clive or not." He looked into the back seat. "But my main priority is to help my youngest daughter find her familiar, who happens to be my friend, too. And then I'd like to enjoy Christmas with my family."

"If I don't see you before tomorrow," said Angus. "Make sure you all have a very merry Christmas."

As they walked towards the medical centre, the twinkling Christmas lights strung across the road beginning to grow brighter as the sun dipped, Millie continued to scan the sky. "I know he's okay," she said. "I'd know if something terrible had happened to him."

"It's Reuben we're talking about," said Judith, regaining her balance as her boot lost grip on the slippery pavement. "He knows how to look after himself, you know that."

"I know," said Millie. "But I can't shake the feeling that even though we neutralised the orb, something still isn't right around here, and it's that *something* which is preventing him from returning."

"Don't worry about that little fella," said Sergeant Spencer, placing a heavy arm around his daughter's shoulders. "Like Judith said — he knows how to look after himself. And he is protected by magic. Never forget that."

Millie knew that. She knew that the real Reuben looked nothing like a cockatiel. She had seen him take on his demon form when she'd visited The Chaos with him. What resided within the cockatiel was Reuben's energy, which had been dragged from The Chaos by the witch who had first rescued him from the awful dimension.

Reuben's strength burned bright within that little bird, and it would take more than a horrible little elf flying on his back to hurt him.

She leaned into her father, his words calming her even though they weren't necessary. She looked up at his rosy red cheeks, stubble beginning to show, even though he'd been freshly shaved when he'd sung Happy Birthday to her that morning. "I know," she said.

As they reached the medical centre, the wrought iron fence decorated in tinsel and a holly wreath hanging on the gate, Sergeant Spencer lifted his arm from Millie's back. "We'll see how Christoph is," he said, "and if Reuben hasn't returned within an hour, we'll turn this town upside down looking for him."

Millie nodded. She looked up as the medical centre door swung open, and shimmering waves of heat poured from the building's warm interior. The nurse they'd met the night before stepped into the cold, wrapping a coat around her shoulders.

She lit a cigarette before she noticed Sergeant Spencer and his daughters. "We were just talking about you three," she said. She took a drag of the cigarette, the tip glowing brightly, and smoke curling through snowflakes. "We were going to send someone to the cabin to get you. You said you wanted to talk to Christoph when he woke up — well, he's awake, but I wouldn't get your hopes up about getting any sense from him. He's confused. We think he might have taken a bang to the head."

"We'll try our best," said Sergeant Spencer, pulling open the heavy gate, the base of it creating a little snowdrift as it dragged across the path.

Then, another voice called out. Millie looked up to see Maggie hurrying across the road towards them, and next to her, Annie, the butcher's wife. Both women dressed against the cold, they stopped a short distance away from the medical centre, out of earshot of the nurse, and waved the three of them over.

"Annie has something to tell you," said Maggie.

Her eyes darting from left to right, and her face pale, Annie rubbed her gloved hands together nervously and took a deep breath. "It's about Clive," she said. "There's something you should know."

"We've already worked it out," said Sergeant Spencer, gently. "Angus told us that Christoph had threatened you. It was Clive that beat Christoph, wasn't it? That's why he left town."

Annie looked confused for a moment and then shook her head quickly. "No!" she said. "Gosh, no! Clive wouldn't hurt a fly! He's a kind man. Yes, he threatened Christoph, but he wouldn't hurt a fly."

"Where was he last night, Annie?" asked Sergeant Spencer. "Are you quite certain he didn't visit Christoph's home?"

"It wasn't Clive that hurt Christoph," interjected Maggie. She took Annie's hand in hers and stared into the scared lady's face. "Tell them. They'll understand. They're like us."

"Clive didn't go to Christoph's home last night," said Annie, in a quiet voice. "He didn't go because he was in his grotto for most of the night, and when he wasn't, he was flying around in his sleigh — getting ready to deliver the presents tonight."

Puzzled, Millie stared at the butcher's wife. "Pardon?"

"Oh, dear!" said Annie. "I did something awful! It was an accident, but I've done something terrible, and I think it's beginning to affect the whole town! There are elves in people's houses!"

"Annie," urged Maggie. "Tell them. Then we can help."

"I'm a witch," confessed Annie. "You're the only people I've ever told, apart from Clive, Maggie and the handful of paranormal people in this town."

"Annie came to me," said Maggie, "and told me what she'd done. She's the cause of all the strange things going on in town."

"But we caused it," said Judith, touching Millie's hand. "The magic we released last night caused it. We've dealt with it, though. We've deactivated it."

"I know," said Maggie. "Angus told me when he came in the pub. I don't think your magic did anything apart from creating a little springtime on the mountainside. Angus told me it was quite spectacular, but I think that's all it was. It's the spell that Annie cast we should be worried about."

"It was an accident," said Annie, through a sob.

Millie reached for Annie's hand and smiled. "We all have accidents, Annie. We won't judge you. Just tell us, so we can help."

Staring at Millie through tears, Annie nodded. "I was making the same eggnog that I make every year. I know I shouldn't, but I always add a little magic. Not enough to raise suspicions, but just enough to lift the spirits of anybody who drinks it. Christmas isn't a happy time of year for everybody, but anybody who takes a sip of my eggnog will have a wonderful Christmas Day."

Recalling how the shot of eggnog had tingled in her throat, Millie smiled. "I thought there was something different about it," she said.

"The magic won't activate properly until tomorrow," explained Annie. "Anybody who drank it will have a day free of any worries or sadness that's affecting them. They'll be able to enjoy Christmas Day."

"Your eggnog has caused elves to appear?" asked Judith.

"Not quite," said the butcher's wife.

"Tell them," urged Maggie.

Annie nodded. "It was silly. Clive and I argued while I was making my eggnog," she explained. "I was adding a little magic to the ingredients when Clive came into the kitchen. He was complaining again that we were selling the turkeys too cheap. I told him that our prices are just fine and that we wanted everybody to be able to afford them, not just people with money. He kept on grumbling, though, and I got fed up. I called him Ebenezer Scrooge, and then he said he felt more like Santa — he said our prices are so cheap he may as well give the turkeys away as Christmas presents." She looked at the floor and then lifted her face, snowflakes drifting past it. "And then it happened."

"What happened?" asked Millie.

"I said, '*I wish you were bloody Santa! Then I'd only have to see you once a year*!'", said Annie. "As I said it, I accidentally released some more magic. I was emotional — I just wanted to enjoy Christmas, but Clive kept whinging about money. We're doing well enough without raising the price of turkeys! The spell mingled with the magic that was already in the eggnog, and there was a flash of light and…" Her voice trailed off, and she sobbed again.

"And?" asked Millie, Annie's hand still in hers.

"Clive was gone!" said Annie. She shook her head. "No. He was still there, but he wasn't Clive anymore. He was Santa! Clive had turned into Santa right before my eyes. Then, he gave a big laugh, sprinkled some sort of magical dust in the air and shouted, 'may all your Christmas dreams come true!'"

"And that's what's happened," said Maggie. "Things that people believe in are coming true."

"And it only takes one person to believe in it to affect everybody in town," said Millie, a horrifying thought embedding itself in her mind. "I have a feeling that things are about to get a little scary if we don't stop it."

"Why do you think that?" asked Annie, her face frozen in an expression of fear.

"Because of the snowmen that are surrounding the town," Millie replied, staring up at the darkening mountain. "We heard a mother telling her son that Santa's evil snowmen would be coming for the naughty children tonight. The only person to believe that story is one little boy — Billy. Yet the snowmen are there, for anyone to see. And they're increasing in number." A chill ran through her, and she pulled her coat tighter. "I knew things still felt wrong, even after Judith and I deactivated our orb. That's why Reuben hasn't come back. Magic must be preventing him."

"We have to stop it!" said Annie. "I don't know what to do! Clive's turned our biggest barn into some sort of awful grotto. He's got an army of elves in there, building wooden toys and singing. I've never been very good at magic — I don't know how to stop it."

"Then let's see if we can," said Millie. "Take us to Santa's Grotto."

"I'll get back to the pub," said Maggie. "If strange things begin to happen in town, my magic might be needed here."

Sergeant Spencer nodded. "Let's go," he said. "Get in the car."

As they hurried past the medical centre, the nurse called out. "Are you going to speak to Christoph?" she asked, stubbing her cigarette out on the wall, tiny red embers falling to the snow at her feet.

"We have a little issue to deal with first," called Sergeant Spencer. "Then we'll speak to him."

Chapter 15

Annie and Clive's large home sat in the belly of a valley on the southern edge of Kilgrettin. Set in extensive grounds, the home consisted of a farmhouse and several outhouses — the largest of which was the size of a regular house.

Instructing Sergeant Spencer to park near the barn, Annie spoke in a nervous voice. "He's in there," she said, pointing at the wooden building. "My magic has turned it into some sort of Christmas nightmare."

Pushing the car door open, Millie stepped outside, snow crunching beneath her feet. "Reuben is near," she said, her familiar's energy strong within her mind. "I can feel him! He's not in the immediate vicinity, but he's not far away!"

"I'm not going in there with you," said Annie, turning her back and striding towards the farmhouse, greeting two black and white collies that ran to her. "I can't bear seeing him like that, and his elves are awful little things. Goddess only knows what my magic has done."

Sergeant Spencer looked at his daughters. "Are you two ready?" he said. "The time to worry about using magic is over. If anything happens inside the barn, don't think twice about casting a spell."

Already two steps ahead of her father, both literally and metaphorically, Millie's fingers tingled with energy as she approached the bright red barn door.

She heard voices before she'd reached the entrance, and recognised them as the same sort of high-pitched voice that the elf on the shelf in Mrs Andrews' home had spoken in. Then, she heard music. As if played on xylophones and cowbells, festive tunes drifted from beneath the tall wooden door.

Reaching the entrance, Millie readied her magic and pushed against the heavy door with her shoulder. Creaking on unoiled hinges, the door moved a little, and Millie pushed harder, making a gap wide enough to fit her head through.

Not prone to gasping, the gasp that left her sounded loud to her ears, but nobody, or nothing, within the barn seemed to have noticed.

Had Annie not warned her about the barn's interior, she may have thought she'd stumbled upon the set of a children's Christmas film.

The struts which supported the roof, which Millie, although no carpenter, assumed should have been made from wood, were colourful poles decorated in spirals of greens, reds and silvers.

Behind a low fence in one corner stood a group of reindeer chewing hay. Barely noticing the flurry of activity around them, they stared aimlessly as they ate. One of the reindeers, a large one with a nose as red as a ripe apple, pushed another of the animals away from a bale of hay and took a large mouthful.

Her eyes widening in astonishment, Millie stared at the large sleigh parked alongside the reindeer's pen. Its paintwork gleaming under the glow of the Christmas lights that hung from every available part of the barn, the sleek work of engineering looked like it had been constructed by the hands of a master craftsman.

Then, she paid attention to the dozens of tiny elves that scurried around the barn. All of them dressed in colourful tights and hats, they sang and laughed as they skipped from place to place, some of them carrying toys made of wood, and some of them eating slabs of cake, which they plucked from the long wooden table which bent under the weight of the Christmas feast which sat upon it.

In one corner, near the tall Christmas tree, a group of elves hammered and sawed pieces of wood. Another dipped a paintbrush into a can of paint and proceeded to colour the face of a wooden doll he cradled in his lap.

"What's happening?" asked Judith from behind her, pushing against Millie's back. "Let me look!"

"Wait a moment," said Millie, her eyes finding the colossal pile of wrapped presents stuffed into bright red sacks, stacked almost as high as the roof.

Then, she saw him — with a group of elves at his feet, some of them singing, and others playing tiny musical instruments. As the elves increased the tempo of their song, Santa Claus lifted his face towards the ceiling and gave a bellowing laugh which echoed around the barn. "Ho! Ho! Ho!"

"Is that him?" asked Judith, excitement in her voice. "Is it him?"

"Yes," whispered Millie. "But I can't see Reuben anywhere."

Then, just as Millie was planning her next move — the decision was made for her. A female elf, her lips caked in thick chocolate, stopped eating the slab of cake she held in her tiny hand and stared at the doorway.

Her little eyes widened, and the bell on her hat jingled as she hopped from foot to foot. Larger than her body, and as high-pitched as an old-fashioned kettle boiling on a gas hob, her voice filled the barn. "Intruders! Intruders!"

As if her voice had flicked a switch, the barn fell into complete silence, only the last vowel of Santa's laugh hovering in the air. All faces turned to the door, and Millie took a deep breath, before pushing the door wider and stepping inside.

The breeze which entered with her made ribbons tied to wooden posts flutter, and even one of the reindeer was distracted from its food, making a deep grunting sound between chews.

With Judith and her father close behind, Millie stepped across the fragrant sawdust scattered on the floor and gazed around.

"Whoa!" said Judith. "I wasn't expecting this."

"It's certainly a sight to behold," said Sergeant Spencer, kicking out in the direction of a plump elf who approached him, menacingly wielding a half-eaten baguette.

"Ho! Ho! Ho!" said the huge man in the red suit, who sat upon his large wooden chair like a king on his throne. He ran a hand through his long silky beard and gave a cheery grin. "Who do we have here?"

With a click of his white-gloved fingers, a large book appeared in his lap. Colourful dust rose from the book as he opened it, and he began flicking through the yellowed pages, peering over gold-rimmed spectacles.

He ran his finger down the page and then chuckled. "Here we are! Millie Thorn, Judith Spencer, and David Spencer. Of course! You three live in the cabin on the hill! I remember, I checked in on you last night, and I'm happy to report that you were all being very good. Millie, you were fast asleep, and Judith and David were putting up Christmas decorations. It made me happy to watch — I stood at the window for a few minutes watching you work."

"It was you looking through people's windows last night?" said Sergeant Spencer.

"Of course!" roared Santa, beckoning them closer. "My elves keep me informed about most people's behaviour, but I can't have an elf in everybody's house! Otherwise, who would make the toys? Ho! Ho! Ho!"

Millie took a step backwards as several elves approached her, staring up at her with distrust.

"Be nice to them, little ones," said Santa. "These ones are nice, not naughty! My snowmen won't be coming for any of these wonderful children."

"We're hardly children," said Judith.

"If your name is on my list," said Santa, closing the book, which vanished in a flash of silver. "Then you're a child in my eyes. And the name of everybody in this town is in my book."

"Come," said an elf with bright red cheeks, who stood at Millie's feet, gazing up at her. "Come closer to Santa."

"Indeed," bellowed Santa. "Come here! Grab some food if you're hungry. There's more than enough to go around, and when that runs out, there will be even more! Nobody goes hungry at Christmas!"

Treading carefully through the throng of elves that scurried alongside her, Millie gazed at the food on the table as she stepped towards Santa.

The feast was impressive. Huge hams, glistening with honey, were placed alongside loaves of freshly baked bread, the warm, yeasty scent mingling with the sweet smell of cinnamon buns and ginger biscuits.

At the centre of the table, golden brown and larger than any she'd seen before, was a turkey. With steam rising from it, and roasted vegetables arranged on the silver platter around it, Millie realised her mouth was watering despite the strange circumstances she found herself in.

Then, with a rush of relief in her heart, she sensed that Reuben was nearer than before, and getting closer as every second passed. As the three of them neared Santa, whose face still wore a broad smile, Millie looked around the barn once more. "Where's my familiar?" she said. "I can feel him. He's near."

"Familiar?" said Santa. "What's a familiar?"

"He's my companion," said Millie. "He's a cockatiel. A little bird."

"Ah, you mean Reuben!" said Santa, his voice reverberating in Millie's ears. "What a wonderful little chap he is! I think he's giving somebody a ride."

"Archie is riding him," said an elf at Santa's feet. "Then it's my turn. Reuben said he'd take me twice around the mountain if I gave him a piece of yule log! I'm going to give him two pieces!"

"Somebody is riding him?" said Millie, her fingers tingling with energy as her rage intensified. "He's not to be ridden. He's my companion. He's my friend. If any of you have harmed a feather on that bird's body, you'll have me to answer to!"

"Nobody's hurt him, missus," said a chubby elf, perched on a wrapped Christmas present. "Only the smallest and lightest of us are riding him. He hurt Freddie, though."

"Indeed," said Santa, looking into the faces of the elves that surrounded him. "Where is Freddie? Is his injury better yet?"

"I'm okay," said a small voice from behind the Christmas tree. Then, a little face that Millie recognised appeared from behind the glitter-coated trunk. "It was quite a scare, though!"

"You!" said Judith. "You're the elf that flew away on Reuben!"

Freddie stepped from behind the tree, his head bowed. "I've already been told off by Santa, and I won't be accompanying him tonight when he delivers the presents. However harshly you scold me — it won't mean a thing. The punishment Santa has given me is punishment enough."

"So, you three are the children that Freddie told me about when Reuben brought him home in his beak," said Santa. He looked at the little elf. "You told me they were naughty children. These are good children — I watched them with my own eyes last night."

Freddie pointed at Sergeant Spencer. "That one tried to touch me and take away my magic. So, I had to escape. It was lucky that Reuben was there — I might never have got out of that room."

"You didn't look very lucky when Reuben brought you home," said another elf, putting a hand to his mouth as he giggled.

"He flew upside down!" said Freddie. "And then

shook me from his back. Then, as I was falling, he grabbed me by the arm. It really hurt! Then, he shouted at me to take him to my leader!"

"And I'm glad you did," said Santa. "He makes a wonderful addition to the family."

"He's already got a family," said Millie. She looked at her sister, and then her father. "We're his family."

Then, distant at first, but rising in volume, came an unmistakable screech. "Ha! We did it! We hit a golden eagle right on the head with a cherry!"

"I threw the cherry," came another high-pitched voice. "You just got us close enough!"

Then, swooping through an open window at the rear of the barn, appeared Reuben. With a tiny elf clinging to his back, he squawked and screeched. "You should have seen that golden eagle! He didn't know what was happening! That cherry bounced right off his bonce!"

Dropping from the air, Reuben swooped low through the barn, skimming the heads of elves, until he made a graceful landing on a Christmas tree branch and whistled as the little elf climbed from his back.

He cocked his head and stared at the three people standing in front of Santa. "You took your time!" he squawked. "Anything could have happened to me!"

"You look fine to me, Reuben," said Millie, stepping towards the tree, scattering elves in her path. "Flying around with elves on your back? Attacking golden eagles? I've been summoning you! Why didn't you come? I was worried about you!"

"I couldn't sense that you were calling me," said Reuben. "There's too much magic in the air. It must have interfered when you tried to summon me. Santa's Christmas magic is heavy in the air, can't you feel it, Millie?"

She could. It was a different sort of magic than she was used to, but it was there, and she recognised it to be the source of the uneasy feeling she'd had about Kilgrettin. "Then why didn't you come to me without me having to summon you?" asked Millie. "They don't seem to be holding you hostage — in fact, you seem to be having quite a jolly old time!"

"I lost track of time," said Reuben, looking away. "I'm sorry. It was such fun! I've been chasing golden eagles. I've been flying to the tops of mountains, and getting paid handsomely for my flying skills in the form of the most amazing food I've ever tasted." He winked in Millie's direction. "No offence meant about your cooking, Millie — but the food on the table was created by magic, and boy, does it taste good!"

"Well, as long as you're safe — that's all that matters," said Millie. She turned her attention to Santa Claus. "Santa," she said. "You are aware that your name is Clive, and that you're a butcher? Your wife is a witch, and she accidentally put a spell on you."

"Ho! Ho! Ho!" guffawed Santa. "Where did you come up with that story? And why would you say such a thing? I'm Santa, and I've chosen this town as my base this year! As long as I'm still here when the clock strikes midnight, I'll be able to stay here forever!"

Millie stared at the sacks of presents stacked high in the corner. "You intend to deliver those presents tonight?"

"Of course!" said Santa. "As soon as it's dark enough, I shall begin my deliveries."

"To the whole world?" asked Millie.

For a moment, Santa's face became confused. Then, he shook his head and spoke. "No," he said. "For some reason, I'll only be delivering in Kilgrettin this year. I don't remember why."

"It's because Annie's magic is contained within the boundaries of this town," said Millie, in a low voice. "At least people outside Kilgrettin won't be reporting sightings of Santa tonight."

"But we can't have Santa flying around Kilgrettin tonight," said Sergeant Spencer, in a low whisper. "Seeing things like that will terrify people. Look what happened to Mrs Andrews, and she only saw a single elf."

His hearing better than Sergeant Spencer had given him credit for, Santa gave a laugh. "There shall be more than just elves in town tonight. Tonight is Christmas Eve! Everybody's beliefs will come true tonight, and Christmas will pass as it's supposed to! Naughty children will be dealt with by my snowmen, so they don't sully Christmas for the good children, and there'll be lots of presents beneath the trees of those who deserve them! It will be a wonderful night!"

"It doesn't sound wonderful for the children you believe have been naughty," noted Sergeant Spencer.

"Ah! That reminds me, David Spencer! I must make an amendment in my book!"

The book appeared in Santa's lap again, and he flicked through the pages. He took a gold pen from his pocket and put it to paper. "David Spencer is naughty, not nice," he murmured as he wrote.

"What?" said Millie's father.

"You tried to touch Freddie the elf," said Santa, the book vanishing with a popping sound. "Every child knows it's naughty to touch an elf on a shelf!"

Sergeant Spencer stepped forward. "But—"

Santa shook his head. "Silence, naughty boy!" he bellowed. "My snowmen will make you think twice about what you did, David."

"I'm not worried about a few snowmen," said Sergeant Spencer.

"Ho! Ho! Ho! Then perhaps I'll send my *very* special helper to deal with you!" bellowed Santa. "He did an excellent job of dealing with an extremely naughty boy last night! Little Christoph Gruber will think twice before doing what he did again!"

"You know what happened to Christoph?" said Millie, sparks flickering at her fingertips.

"Of course," said Santa. "It's what he wanted. It's what he believed in!"

"What did you do?" shouted Millie, sparks

cascading to the floor around her.

His large wooden chair creaking, Santa got to his feet and pointed a gloved hand at Millie. "Put that away!" he demanded. As he spoke, a tendril of energy, coloured like a Christmas ribbon left his fingertip and snaked a route towards her.

It moved quickly, and before Millie could respond, had wrapped itself around her wrist, draining the magic from her hand. "Ouch!" she said, as the ribbon uncoiled itself from her flesh and sped towards Judith.

A spell aimed at Santa leaving her hand, Judith cried out in pain as the ribbon wrapped her wrist in colourful coils, the sparks she'd conjured dropping to the sawdust floor, where they flickered and vanished.

"All three of you are naughty children," said Santa. "Freddie was right! You have some sort of magic, too! Your magic won't work here, though! There's Christmas magic in the air! Can't you feel it? My Christmas magic is far more powerful than anything you two naughty children could ever produce.

"Now, I'd like you to leave my grotto. You're not welcome here, and I'm considering sending my very special helper to deal with you girls. I think you deserve more than my snowmen; you've been *very* naughty indeed! My special helper will be very busy tonight. He's already on his way to make sure that Christoph is behaving tonight, and when he's finished watching that greedy child, I'll send him to deal with you two!"

Then, as Santa raised a hand, the barn filled with light, and Millie's ears popped. The temperature dropped, and she felt a breeze on her face. Opening her eyes, she realised she was no longer in the barn. She was standing outside in the snow, staring at the barn door, a cold wind biting her ears.

"That was quite a trick," said Judith, from beside Millie. "He transported us."

Sergeant Spencer reached for the barn door and abruptly withdrew his hand as air hissed through his teeth. "Ow. There's some sort of force field," he said.

"He's locked you out," squawked Reuben, fluttering from an open window above them.

"But he's let you go," said Millie. "Thank goodness."

"He's not bad," said Reuben, landing on Millie's shoulder. "He's acting on instinct. Everything he does is fuelled by the Christmas beliefs of people in this town, not his own vindictiveness."

"You heard what he said, Reuben," said Judith. "He knows what happened to Christoph. He's responsible for what happened to the poor man."

"Not exactly," said Sergeant Spencer. "He said it was his very special helper — whoever that is."

"And he also said that his helper was on his way to visit Christoph again," said Millie, hurrying towards the car. "We have to get there. Santa's helper beat Christoph almost to death last night. He won't survive another ordeal like that!"

Chapter 16

Driving within the limits that the weather permitted, Sergeant Spencer concentrated on the road, the car's headlights slicing through the gloom.

Her fingers on the door handle, Millie stiffened in her seat, remembering the near miss they'd had the day before. She felt for her magic, ready to cast a spell if she sensed the car was about to leave the road. She frowned and tried again. *Nothing.* Her magic felt strange, like a battery drained of power.

She turned to her sister. "Is your magic responding?"

Judith concentrated for a moment and then shook her head. "No. It feels weak. Santa must've drained it with that ribbon he attacked us with. I can feel it recovering, but it's going to take a little time."

"Then let's hope we won't be needing magic any time soon," said Millie.

As the SUV turned into the market square, relief washed over Millie as she took in her surroundings. Everything appeared normal. Nobody ran through the streets terrorised by elves. Santa was nowhere to be seen, and there was no sign of a mysterious special helper.

Drawing the vehicle to a halt outside the medical centre, Sergeant Spencer leapt out, snowflakes immediately collecting in his hair. "I've got a bad feeling," he said, his breath rising as he stared around the square.

Millie looked, too. Shop windows illuminated the pavements with festive window displays, and a fox scampered from an alley, leaving tiny footsteps in the snow as it crossed the road. Two adults and a child stood at a nativity scene, constructed in a makeshift wooden stable, and the Christmas lights strung across the road cycled slowly through a kaleidoscope of Christmas hues.

Despite the peacefulness, and despite the perfect Christmas image that the town centre portrayed, Millie still experienced the same sense of dread that her father had spoken of.

A shiver ran through her, and it was nothing to do with the cold. She followed her father and sister through the gate in the fence surrounding the medical centre and felt for her magic again. It was stronger, but still not strong enough.

She looked at Judith as her father opened the door, a blast of heat hitting her, doing nothing to remove the chill of dread in her bones. "Be careful," she warned. "If this so-called special helper is here, we saw what it did to Christoph last night. It's dangerous."

Judith nodded, flexing her hand, a look of concern in her eyes when no sparks appeared at her fingertips. "Santa promised he was sending it after us, too," she said.

Sergeant Spencer faced his daughters. "I might not possess magical powers," he said. "But I promise you both this — I'll fight anything that tries to hurt either of you. You have my word." Standing half in and half out of the building, he narrowed his eyes. "I'm going in here because I'm a police officer. I need to speak to Christoph. The helper that Santa spoke of may or may not make an appearance, but you two both know you don't have to come in there with me, don't you?"

Gazing at her father's face, his eyes gleaming with fierce stoicism, Millie smiled. "Families stick together," she said, pushing past her father into the sterile light of the corridor. "However hard things get."

"I agree," said Judith, stepping into the building after Millie, brushing snow from her hair. "We've dealt with worse things than anything I imagine a large, unshaven man in a red shell suit could throw at us. Anyway, who do you think his special helper is? Some sort of elf? One that's far bigger than the others?"

A little voice came from Millie's coat. "You make

sure you keep it off my back! I don't want some fat bugger back there! I'm still tender!"

Her fingers brushing soft feathers, Millie slid a hand into her pocket. "You were taken from me once today, Reuben," she said. "I won't let it happen again."

"Good," said Reuben. "Because to be quite frank — I'm really not enjoying our Scottish Christmas vacation. I'd intended to be feasting on cheese and crackers tonight while watching Die Hard. This is not how you sold this trip to me, Millie. I did warn you all, though. I tried to tell you — Scotland is not a pleasant place!"

As Millie folded the flap of her pocket over the little bird's complaints, the raised voice of a man drifted along the corridor. Then, a woman shouted, her voice urgent.

"Come on," said Millie, hurrying along the corridor, heading for the room they'd left Christoph in the night before.

Her boots squeaking on tiles, she hurried past the water cooler and vending machine, and pushed open the door to Treatment Room Number Two. Not knowing what to expect on the other side, she felt for her magic again, frustrated when it responded with only a tingle of weak energy.

The nurse standing next to Christoph's bed looked at the door in shock. "You gave me a fright! What do you think you're doing — barging in here like that?"

"We came to see if Christoph was okay," said Judith. "We heard shouting."

"Christoph just woke up," said the nurse. "The doctor had to put him back to sleep when he regained consciousness earlier today. He kept trying to get out of bed — fighting us and shouting some nonsense about monsters."

"It's true!" yelled the thin man in the bed, his words shaped by a Germanic accent. "He's a monster! I want to go! Let me out of this bed!"

"No!" said the nurse, leaning over him and placing a hand on each of his arms. "You have to stay in bed, Christoph! You're weak. You must stay here until you're well! Somebody almost killed you last night. If you don't calm down, I'll call for the doctor — and he'll give you another sedative!"

Christoph struggled against the nurse, and she glanced over her shoulder. "Would somebody help me?" she asked. "I don't want him to hurt himself."

Millie hurried to the bed and leaned over Christoph, placing both hands on the arm the nurse released. With somebody holding each of his arms, the already weak man struggled a little and then relaxed. "You have to believe me," he said, his voice hoarse. "He came for me! Because I was naughty!"

Her concern about whether the man would live or die having been the critical issue, Millie hadn't taken much notice of Christoph's appearance the night before. She stared down at him, her eyes making contact with his.

Angus had said the man was a criminal, but that didn't mean he was an inherently bad man. His eyes were kind — pale blue, made bluer by his greying eyebrows and the soft wrinkles on his forehead.

His lips, dried by dehydration, trembled as he gazed back at Millie. Managing to move his hand, he clutched Millie's coat and pulled her closer to him. "You must believe me!" he rasped.

Relaxing her grip on his arm, Millie smiled. "I do," she said. "Tell me about the monster."

"Don't encourage him," said the nurse. "You'll set him off again."

As Christoph stared at Millie, a glazed look slid across his face, and his eyes seemed to lose focus. His cheeks, already devoid of colour, turned whiter.

The nurse grabbed a little pouch from a table alongside the bed and unzipped it. She fiddled with the contents, and then took Christoph's hand in hers. She pressed a plastic device against his fingertip, drawing a droplet of blood.

Applying the droplet to a small device with a screen, she waited for a few seconds and then dropped the patient's hand. "He's diabetic," she explained. "His blood sugars are low." She hurried towards an open door opposite the bed. "Don't worry, Christoph," she shouted, over the chinking of crockery. "We'll soon have you feeling better."

Christoph's eyes darted left and right as he attempted to focus on Millie. His breathing slowed. "I don't feel well," he slurred.

"I'm coming," said the nurse, hurrying to the bed with a plate in her hand.

Picking up an iced cookie in the shape of a Christmas tree, she snapped the tip from the tree and placed it at Christoph's lips. "Eat this," she said, pushing it into his mouth. "We need to get your sugars up quickly. This will make you feel better, and then I'll make you a nice sandwich."

His eyes closed, Christoph moved his mouth slowly as he chewed.

"How long will it take to work?" said Judith.

The nurse popped another piece of the festive cookie into Christoph's mouth. "It'll be quick," she said.

As Christoph chewed on a third piece of cookie, colour rising in his cheeks, he opened his eyes and stared at Millie. "That's better," he mumbled.

Peeling open a small packet, the nurse squeezed some of the contents into Christoph's mouth. "Glucose gel," she said, smiling at Judith.

As Christoph sucked on the gel, his eyes regained even more focus, and suddenly he seemed to recall that he didn't want to be there.

He began struggling, kicking his legs as he attempted to stand up. "I want to go! It might come back. I want to leave this town!"

"Stay there!" said the nurse, gently pushing him onto the mattress. "I'm not trying to be nasty — you're not well, Christoph! You must stay in bed!"

Twisting his head, Christoph stopped struggling as his eyes fell on the plate next to his bed.

He slowly turned to the nurse, fear etched in every crease of his face. "You gave me one of those Christmas treats?" he said.

"Yes," said the nurse. "A biscuit. To help get your sugars back to normal. When you stop struggling, I'll make you a nice sandwich."

"But it's not Christmas Day," sobbed Christoph. "I'm not allowed to eat Christmas treats until Christmas Day! Mama always told me what would happen if I ate treats before Christmas Day, but I never believed her!"

The fear in Christoph's eyes contagious, Millie licked her dry lips. "Tell me, Christoph," she coaxed. "What happens if you eat treats before Christmas Day?"

Christoph's eyes darted around the room, as if he were looking for something. He struggled with Millie and the nurse once more and then sobbed. "Mama and Papa were poor! Christmas is very important in Austria, but Mama and Papa couldn't afford to spend lots of money on Christmas treats! They told us what would happen if we ate any before Christmas Day! They warned us who would come! I never believed them! I thought it was a story they told to stop my brother and me from eating the Christmas food. I'd forgotten all about the stories they used to tell us, until yesterday! Until he came!"

"Until who came?" asked Sergeant Spencer.

"I cut a piece of stollen," said Christoph, choosing not to answer the question. "It's my favourite. But I shouldn't have! I shouldn't have cut a piece until Christmas Day!" He sobbed again and stared at the plate next to his bed. "And now you've made me eat another Christmas treat! He told me he'd come back if I were a naughty boy again! And now I've eaten another one, he'll come back and beat me with the stick he uses on naughty children."

"Who'll come back?" said Judith, staring nervously around the room.

"He's confused," said the nurse, smiling at Judith. "He's traumatised from the beating that some awful person gave him yesterday. Poor man." She smiled at Christoph. "It's okay. Nobody is coming to get you. You're perfectly safe here."

His mouth opening slowly, and his body becoming rigid, Christoph let out a scream that reverberated off the white walls. He screamed again and kicked his legs. Then, he stared across the room, past Millie's head, his eyes frozen in a horrified stare. "It's too late," he said, pointing a trembling finger. "He's here."

"There's nobody here," said the nurse. She twisted her head in the direction Christoph was pointing. "Look —" she began.

Then, her whole body shook. As her legs gave way beneath her, she let out a whimper as she slumped to the floor. "What is it?" she moaned.

Judith was already backing towards the door as

Millie turned her head with trepidation, terrified of what she might see.

As Sergeant Spencer placed himself in front of Judith and stepped past Millie, Christoph mumbled two words. "It's Krampus."

Chapter 17

"What's a Krampus?" said Sergeant Spencer, placing himself between his daughters and the hideous creature which forced its way through the wall, as if the building were giving birth to it.

"It's a European tradition," stammered Judith. "Santa deals with good children, and Krampus punishes the naughty ones."

Fear holding her feet to the floor, Millie watched in horror as the elongated face of the creature pushed itself into the room. The wall around it flowed like liquid, and it thrust a clawed hand towards them, shaking the thick rusty chains coiled around its wrist. "Somebody's been a naughty boy," it growled, its voice loud and menacing. "What did I tell you last night, Christoph?"

The red leathery flesh of its distorted face twisted

as it opened its mouth, revealing long fangs and a serpentine tongue which flicked at the air. "I can taste Christmas treats! You know you're not supposed to eat Christmas treats until Christmas Day, Christoph! Mama and Papa told you so!"

Retreating along the bed, until he was a trembling ball pressed tightly against the headboard, Christoph spoke through ragged sobs. "That was fifty years ago, Krampus!" he pleaded, tears falling from his cheeks. "Mama and Papa are dead! They don't care if I eat Christmas treats!"

"But I care!" roared Krampus, pushing more of his body through the wall, a black hoof scraping the tiled floor as he pushed a leg into the room. "I care very much, little Christoph!"

The beast's head, adorned with scaled horns, contorted as it spoke. Its eyes shifted position, and its face changed shape as if it were melting in the heat of a fire.

As its second hoof clicked on the hard floor, it stood to its full height, its horns brushing the ceiling, and a rough hessian sack gripped in the long fingers of one hand.

It rattled the chains again and roared with laughter as the nurse scrambled to her feet and headed for the door, slipping and sliding as she made her escape. It yelled after her. "The snowmen are waiting for you outside, Jemima. You've been a very naughty girl! Santa knows that you put both yourself and your husband on a diet, but you've been eating Christmas treats, while your husband has been eating the food that he hates! You naughty, selfish girl!"

As Jemima pushed through the door, her hospital clogs squeaking on the floor, she stared at Krampus and gave another scream.

As the door swung closed behind her, Krampus shook his chains and extended his tongue, slime dripping from it as he flicked it in Millie's direction. "Millie Thorn and Judith Spencer," he hissed. "You two have been naughty, too! Santa told me what you did — you tried to use magic in his grotto! When I've dealt with Christoph, I'll deal with you!"

Stepping nearer the beast, Sergeant Spencer tilted his chin and looked up into the snarling face. "Over my dead body," he said.

Millie's nostrils twitched as a foul stench poured from the creature. A sickly mix of rotting leaves and decaying flesh, it quickly filled the small room. She felt for her magic again, but instead of surging energy in her arm, she felt something wriggling against her hip.

Then, pushing himself from Millie's pocket, Reuben thrust himself forward in a flurry of feathers. "Over my dead body, too!" he screeched.

His jaundiced eyes sliding through his leathery flesh, Krampus followed the cockatiel's progress as it fluttered around the room. Then, he lowered his snout and gazed at Sergeant Spencer. "Ha!" he roared. "If that's the way you want it, that's the way it will be. I can quite easily transform you into a dead body which I'll step over."

Lowering the dirty hessian sack to the floor, Krampus opened the neck and reached inside. He looked at Christoph. "You know what's in here, don't you?"

His eyes wild, and his body trembling, Christoph spoke as if in shock. "The stick you use to beat naughty children," he said as if answering a general knowledge question.

"Indeed," said Krampus, his hand emerging from the sack, a knotted length of wood gripped in his fist. "My trusty piece of blackthorn. You felt its sting last night, didn't you, Christoph?"

"Yes," said Christoph. "It hurt!"

"It's supposed to hurt!" roared Krampus, spittle hurtling from his mouth. "That's what naughty children deserve!"

As Krampus withdrew the weapon, the stick far too long for the seemingly bottomless sack it emerged from, Millie took a step towards him. She tried in vain to pluck some magic from her chest, but only a useless dribble of energy ran the length of her arm. "We won't let you hurt our father," she said. "We won't let you hurt anybody."

"And how are you going to stop me?" bellowed Krampus, his bicep bulging as he gripped the length of wood.

Without warning, his hooves clicking on tiles, and

his head bowed, Krampus strode towards Millie, the stick lifted, ready to swing.

"Don't you dare!" shouted Millie's father, placing himself between daughter and beast. He lifted a hand as the stick moved in a lethal arc, the air around it throbbing as it cut a path towards Millie's head.

The force with which Krampus swung the stick connected with Sergeant Spencer's body as he took the blow for his daughter.

Making a sickening thudding sound as wood slammed into his chest, the policeman's breath left him in an awful gasp, and his body crumpled as the force of the blow launched him from his feet.

His arms flailing, he thudded into a wheeled trolley. Slamming into a wall, the trolley spilt its cargo, scattering syringes across the floor. Groaning, Sergeant Spencer lay in a heap, his face white and his eyes closed.

"Dad!" yelled Millie, approaching her father.

"Watch out, Millie!" squawked Reuben.

She heard the stick before she saw it, and sidestepped the blow as Krampus swung for her. He roared with malevolent laughter as he drew the stick behind himself again, his muscles bulging as he prepared to attack once more.

Her face red with rage, Judith grabbed an IV pole from alongside Christoph's bed and drew it behind her, swinging it in a wide arc as she screamed at the monster. "My father! You hurt my father!"

The aluminium pole thudded against the tough

hide of the monster, eliciting a roaring laugh from it. "You'll wish you hadn't done that, you naughty little girl!"

Hurtling at Krampus's head, Reuben screeched as he clawed at the monster's face, his beak aimed at its soulless eyes.

"Be careful, Reuben!" shouted Millie.

As Reuben pecked at his leathery face, Krampus moved with alarming speed. Snatching the bird from the air in a clawed hand, he stared at the cockatiel, before placing it in his sack.

The neck of the sack forming a knot without his help, Krampus smiled. "I'll be hungry after dealing with you petulant children. The bird will make a welcome snack."

Turning his attention back to the witches, Krampus closed on them, his stick ready for another attack. He glanced at Christoph, who trembled on the bed. "You stay there," he warned. "When I've dealt with these wicked children, I'll deal with you!"

Struggling desperately to find her magic, Millie stepped away from the creature, aware that he stood between her and the door. Her magic was almost there, growing stronger by the second. It wasn't enough though, and as Krampus snarled, his fangs glinting, Millie shook her head in despair.

Her father lay broken on the ground. Her familiar had been taken from her again, and she and her sister were about to be bludgeoned by the huge stick which Krampus prepared to swing.

She'd let them down. Her magic was more powerful than Judith's. Judith was the big sister, but Millie was the guardian. It was Millie's job to defend her family, and she'd failed them all.

A tear bulged at the corner of her eye as Krampus sneered at her, the foul stench of his breath heavy in the air.

She'd almost lost her family yesterday, but she'd managed to save them from death. This wasn't a car accident, though, and her magic was weak. Judith's magic was weak. Two sisters. Two witches. Both too weak to defend one another.

Then, as cautiously as a soldier lifting his head above the walls of a trench, she allowed herself a sliver of hope. *Maybe, just maybe!*

Reaching for her sister's hand, she forced what little magic she could muster along her arm. "We have to do it together!" she said. "Like last night, when we made the orb!"

Judith's response came in the form of gentle energy which throbbed against Millie's palm. As Krampus bore down on them, his eyes vindictive and cruel, she plucked as much energy as she could from her chest, sending it to her hand.

When she'd given all that she could, she looked at Judith as Krampus's stick began its arc towards them. "Imagine he can't move!" she yelled.

She lifted her hand, bringing her sister's with it as if she were a referee and Judith was a victorious boxer.

Then, as if Judith were replenishing an empty battery within her, Millie's hand danced with energy. She squeezed her sister's fingers tighter, and then she shouted. "Now!"

Sparks burst from the girl's clasped hands, and as the stream of energy rushed to meet Krampus, she shouted the instructions she wanted from the magic. "Make him be still!"

As the bolt of magic thudded into Krampus's broad chest, the creature groaned, the swing of his heavy stick stopping inches from Judith's head. He stopped blinking, and his ragged breathing became softer.

"I don't know how long the spell will last," said Millie, dropping her sister's hand. "We have to get Reuben out of that sack and get Dad and Christoph out of here!"

Nodding, Judith rushed for her father. "Dad?" she said. "Are you all right?"

"I've felt better," grunted Sergeant Spencer, attempting to push himself from the ground.

He stared up at Krampus, who stood silent and still, only the twitching corner of one eye and the infrequent rise and fall of his chest belying the fact he was alive.

Millie joined her sister alongside their father, and both girls gripped him beneath an arm. "You have to stand up, Dad," said Millie.

Sergeant Spencer nodded, and allowing the girls

to take his weight, managed to get to his feet, groaning as he straightened his legs.

"I can manage him on my own," said Judith. "You get Reuben." She looked at Christoph. "Come on! Time to go!"

Staring blankly at Judith, Christoph climbed to the edge of the bed and put a bare foot on the floor. With the hospital gown he wore revealing his naked buttocks and the bandaged wounds on his back, he hurried towards the door without casting a single glance over his shoulder.

As the doors closed behind him, Sergeant Spencer grunted. "And without even giving us a thank you, he's gone," he said.

Staring into the yellowed eyes of the awful Christmas monster which loomed over her, Millie wasn't surprised that Christoph had escaped at the first chance he'd been given. Unlike her and her family, Christoph was not used to seeing paranormal beings, especially monsters formed from his childhood beliefs. She imagined that had she been in the unfortunate man's position, she would have run away too.

Ignoring the immobilised eyes of Krampus, Millie reached for the dirty hessian sack on the floor. Tugging at one end of the knot which tied the neck, she stared at Judith in horror. "I can't open it!" she said. "The knot won't budge. I think it's affected by our spell as much as Krampus is!"

"Then bring it with you," said Judith. "We have to get out of here before the magic wears off."

Gripping the rough fabric, Millie lifted. She tried again, using every ounce of strength she possessed. As if it were loaded with bricks, the sack remained resiliently grounded. "It won't budge! I think the spell we cast is preventing it from moving!"

Then, from the corner of her eye, she saw one of Krampus's nostrils quiver. Then a finger moved on the stick which remained poised to strike. She looked at Judith and pointed at the door. "Go!" she ordered. "Get Dad out of here. Find Maggie — she'll still have magic. She might be able to defeat Krampus."

"What are you going to do?" asked Judith.

"I'm going to wait here until the spell has worn off," said Millie, her eye on the sack which contained her familiar. "When Krampus can move again, I'll be able to open his sack. I'm going to release Reuben and make a run for it."

Seeing a thousand thoughts flicker through her sister's eyes before she made her decision, Millie relaxed a little as her sister nodded. *At least they'd escape.*

Judith gave her sister a thin smile. "I'll see you soon," she said. "Be careful, Millie." Then she stared at Krampus. "He's waking up — Dad and I will get help."

"No," said Sergeant Spencer, pain on his face as he put weight on an injured leg. "I won't leave you here with that thing!"

Millie pointed at the door. "Go!" she said. "When Krampus wakes up, I have to be quick. I can't release

Reuben from the sack *and* make sure you can get out. Look at you, you can hardly walk!"

"But —"

"But nothing," said Millie, cutting off her father's sentence. "Just go. The longer you stay here, the less time you'll have to get me some help. Even when I've released Reuben, Krampus still has to be dealt with — you need to go and find somebody who can help us!"

Blowing out a long breath and nodding slowly, her father relented. "Be careful, Millie," he said, and then limped alongside Judith as they made for the door. "I wish your birthday had turned out differently."

"I've spent it with people I love," said Millie, bringing a hand to her pendant. "That's all that matters."

As the door closed behind them, and their muffled footsteps decreased in volume, Millie stood next to the sack, waiting for the spell to lift. With every second that passed, Krampus appeared to gain more control over his body.

The frequency of his breaths increased, and he made a strange gurgling sound in his throat as he tried to speak. He flexed his large fingers over the stick, and his numerous eyes swivelled to stare at Millie.

Then, as if released from a mould, he stumbled, the momentum of the swing he'd been taking catching him off balance.

Grasping the sack, Millie tried to lift it. Resisting

the force she applied, it slid away from her, moving closer to Krampus. Panic in her throat, she clenched her teeth and tried once more, tugging at the dirty material. It was no use, she realised with angry frustration — the sack was bonded by magic to Krampus.

Giving up on lifting the sack, she concentrated on opening it, digging a nail into the hessian, pulling the knot apart. Aware that Krampus had fully recovered, and was turning to face her, Millie picked at the final piece of hessian holding the sack closed.

As the material gave way, she pulled the neck open. As she prepared to reach inside and rescue Reuben, Krampus roared with awful laughter and pointed his stick at the sack.

Ripping itself from her hand, the neck of the sack tied itself again, this time in a double knot — the bonds pulling tight.

"Only I decide what gets put in my sack, and what gets taken out of it," bellowed Krampus. "It's time you learned a lesson, you naughty, naughty girl! You've really overstepped the mark today!"

Stepping towards her, the stench of his breath in the air, he lifted his stick and brought it down like an executioner swinging an axe. The edge of the stick thudding off her shoulder and sending her sprawling to the floor, Millie gasped in pain but managed to avoid what would have been a fatal blow which was aimed at her head.

Hoping against hope that she could muster some magic, she clawed at the empty spot in her chest —

frustrated and angry when there was no response. Her shoulder throbbing, she scrambled to her feet, dodging another powerful swing of the stick.

Fuelled by a newfound rage, Krampus rushed at Millie, catching her off-guard, gripping her hair in a clawed hand which scratched at her scalp. As if she weighed no more than his sack, he lifted her from the floor, her hands wrapped around his cold forearm, struggling to take the weight off her hair follicles. Aware she was screaming, she kicked at the monster, tears of pain stealing her vision.

"I've had enough of you!" screamed Krampus, his breath hot on Millie's face.

As he bellowed with rage, Krampus lifted Millie higher in the air. When she could feel the ceiling beneath her knuckles, he slammed her to the floor, ripping hair from her scalp as he withdrew his hand.

Her body aching, Millie stared through watering eyes at the blurred image above her. Perhaps it was merciful that she couldn't make out the details as Krampus loomed over her. Maybe it would be best that she didn't see the blow coming.

Even through tears, she saw the shape of the stick rising. Then Krampus roared, his stinking spittle joining the tears that wet Millie's face. "I'm afraid you won't be having a very merry Christmas!" he said.

She sensed his body tensing, and she heard the air throbbing as the stick moved. As she prepared herself, hoping it would be quick, she heard another noise. A noise that reverberated through the room, making her skin tingle.

Then it came again — the guttural roar of an angry animal.

Chapter 18

Bouncing off the walls and floor, the terrifying sound shook Millie into action. Aware that Krampus's attention had been taken off her, she wiped tears from her face with the back of her hand, regaining her vision.

As Krampus lifted himself to his full height, Millie scrambled backwards, watching the newcomer to the fray as it thrust itself at the monster, gaining momentum as it moved.

Millie had understood what it was the moment she'd heard the roar. She was no stranger to were-wolves — she'd seen plenty of seemingly normal men and women transform into terrifying beasts.

As she watched the werewolf, in the final stages of its transformation as it hurtled towards Krampus, she knew she'd never seen one so large. Its face, still recog-nisable as Angus, elongated and twisted as it changed into the head of a fearsome beast. The animal's limbs bulged with muscle beneath the coarse fawn hair, and its eyes glowed a vicious amber.

The werewolf roared again, its face losing the last of its humanity as the transformation was completed, shredded clothing dropping from its body.

Taken off-guard, Krampus stepped backwards, his stick held before him. He tensed his body, preparing himself for the imminent collision with hundreds of pounds of snarling animal.

With razor-sharp claws extended, Angus gave another roar of rage and slammed into the hooved creature.

The loud thump of muscle on muscle shook the air around Millie. She scrambled further backwards as Krampus emitted a hideous howl, the impact of Angus sending him hurtling across the room.

Plaster crumbled from the wall as the massive beast cannonballed into it, and as the claws on Angus's hind legs searched for purchase on the tiled floor, it shook its head in anger.

Millie ran to the sack as the two creatures wrestled, but cursed silently as she tried to open it. It continued to refuse her entry, the greasy knot twisting tighter as she attempted to pick it apart.

Angus gave a vicious growl, and Millie turned from the sack as the werewolf aimed a bite at Krampus's face.

Managing to evade the full force of the bite, Krampus hissed as one of Angus's long fangs grazed his cheek, slicing a flap of flesh from his grotesque face. His stick clattering to the floor as he used his own claws to stab and slash at the wolf, he emitted a terrifying screech of anger.

Digging the claws of his front paws into Krampus's broad shoulders, Angus lifted his hind legs to Krampus's leathery abdomen, and in an attempt at disemboweling his opponent, pierced the tough flesh with his claws, dragging them towards the floor.

Flesh parted, and Krampus screamed as the werewolf's claws exposed the bone in his thigh.

Tugging at the sack in frustration, Millie searched fruitlessly for her magic once more, her eardrums stinging as Krampus howled in rage, the wound in his thigh opening further.

As Krampus stumbled, blood spilling from his leg, Angus dug his claws further into his shoulders. He dragged his enemy from the wall, moving his face to within easy biting distance.

As Angus snapped at Krampus, his teeth grazing and slicing flesh, Millie watched on in horror. An unwilling spectator, held in place by her fear for the safety of both Reuben and Angus.

Then her horror turned to a colder fear than the one already seeping through her bones. She'd assumed that Angus would beat Krampus in a battle of strength, but something was happening to Krampus. Something that would give him an unfair advantage.

The wounds on Krampus's body had begun closing. His thick hide drew across the wounds and blood stopped flowing. He appeared to gain strength as his wounds healed, and he pushed against Angus as the werewolf continued to pull him.

Taken off balance, his hind legs without grip on the tiles, the wolf slid to the floor.

"Angus!" shouted Millie. "Get up!"

Slamming a foot into the werewolf's head, his hoof cracking against Angus's skull, Krampus roared with laughter. "It came to save you!" he said, looking at Millie. "And when I've killed it, It'll be your turn!"

Facedown and flailing on the floor, blood seeped from the wound on Angus's head. Krampus lifted his hoof once more, slamming it into the wolf.

The wolf howled in pain, and Krampus grabbed him with big hands, flipping him onto his back as if he weighed nothing. With his back to the door, he unwrapped the chain from his wrist and twisted it around the wolf's thick neck. He stared at Millie as he began drawing it tight, the clink of metal accompanying the gargling struggles of the wolf.

"Get off him!" screamed Millie, searching desperately for her magic, rage and panic bubbling inside her.

Balling both hands into fists, she ran at the monster. Her hands stinging as they made contact, she delivered blow after blow to his back as he continued to tighten the chain around Angus's neck, laughing mercilessly as he did so.

Sobbing with anger and frustration, Millie kicked, scratched and hit Krampus. Aside from the pain it inflicted on her, she may as well have been hitting empty air. Her attack had no effect on the monster.

Unflinching as Millie continued her assault, the beast looked towards the ceiling. It roared as Angus gurgled and gasped, his arms now limp and his eyes rolling in his skull.

"Please!" screamed Millie, resorting to begging. "Please don't kill him!"

Ignoring her pleas, Krampus breathed heavily as he twisted the chain, the stench of his breath turning Millie's stomach.

Never having felt so weak, so flawed, so helpless — Millie wept as the wolf lay still.

Then, as she prepared for Krampus to turn on her, the door slammed open, and Christoph appeared, his face set in a determined scowl.

He stared at Millie, his eyes alive with anger, and then he turned to the beast standing over the limp wolf.

"You don't scare me!" he yelled, rushing at Krampus, his hospital robe giving him no dignity.

"You came back for your punishment!" roared Krampus. "Are you ready for your beating?"

As Christoph neared Krampus, he looked to his left, and like a dancer on ice, swiftly changed direction. "You can't beat me without your stick!" he shouted.

Krampus stared at his hands, and then at the floor where his stick lay, knocked from his grip during the struggle. "Don't you touch that!" he roared.

But Christoph already had. Struggling to lift the heavy weapon, Christoph's arms trembled under the strain as he lifted the stick above his head.

Screaming his anger, Krampus towered over the man, spittle falling on Christoph like rain. "Give me my stick!"

Christoph shook his head. "No!" he yelled, pulling the stick behind him like a cricket player preparing to swing a bat. "I won't. I'm not scared of you!"

"You should be!" roared Krampus, a clawed hand swiping at Christoph.

Nimble on his feet, Christoph took a step to the side, and then with pure anger etched on his features, he swung the stick at his adversary's head. "I like Christmas treats!" he yelled. "And I'm going to have them whenever I want! You're not real!"

At first, Krampus sneered as the piece of blackthorn slammed into the side of his twisted face, but then, his eyes flickered with new emotions. *Fear and uncertainty*.

He opened his mouth to speak, but his jaw fell open, slack — as if no longer attached by muscle or tendon.

Then, he stumbled, colourful dust rising from the wound Christoph had inflicted on his face.

"What have you done?" he mumbled, staggering backwards, lifting a hand to his face.

"You were here because of what I believed!" shouted Christoph, swinging the stick again, slamming it into Krampus's chest. "And I don't believe I'm scared of you anymore! It's time for you to go! I left you behind fifty years ago. You have no right to be here now! You were just a silly story my Mama and Papa told me."

"But you must still believe in me," said Krampus, his words slurred. "Otherwise, I wouldn't be here."

"Maybe somewhere in the back of my mind!" yelled Christoph. "Maybe when I cut that piece of stollen, I remembered the stories my parents used to tell me. But that doesn't mean I believe in you! I want you to go!"

Another wound opened on Krampus's face as Christoph landed a fresh blow, and more colourful dust rose from the gash. Recognising it as identical to the dust that had risen from Santa's book, Millie understood what was happening. The magic which had created Krampus no longer had an anchor in the world, Christoph had denied his belief, and the beast was dying.

As Krampus roared again, his whole body crumbling beneath him, a cloud of sparkling Christmas dust replacing the stench of his awful breath, Millie ran to Angus's side as the wolf's body began shifting to its human form.

Knowing that when a wolf died, it immediately reverted to human, Millie searched for magic within her. Expecting nothing, she gasped when her chest tingled.

Then, the heat in her chest grew, and she forced it through her body. As Krampus crumbled to nothing, a distant scream accompanying his demise, Millie realised what was happening.

The magic that had created Krampus was magic like any other, and the particles of dust in the air were potent energy. She knew that magic without a home would search for a host. Although Millie's magic had been weak, it had been strong enough to attract the nearby particles.

Confidence rising with her magic, she turned to the wolf. As coarse hair retreated into Angus's flesh, and his bones cracked as his body shrunk, Millie concentrated hard.

Already accomplished at casting healing spells, she prayed she was strong enough to save the life of the man who had been willing to sacrifice his own life to save hers.

Laying her hand on his chest, Millie closed her eyes and concentrated. Using everything she'd learned since she'd discovered she was a witch, she sent healing thoughts riding on the back of powerful energy which surged through the unconscious man.

With her eyes still closed, she narrowed in on her thoughts. Then she pushed more energy into Angus. Ordering his heart to beat. Demanding that his lungs inflate with air. Begging his body to work.

Then she heard it, a soft whisper. "You're not so bad for a wee lassie from the South of England."

Opening her eyes, Millie let out the breath she didn't know she'd been holding. She stared into

Angus's eyes, which sparkled with life. Her spell had been strong. "Are you okay?"

"I've never felt better," said Angus, his beard now insignificant in comparison to the thick hairs that had covered his body. "Where did the beastie go? Did you kill it?"

"No," said Millie, rushing to the sack which now lay open on the floor. She smiled at Christoph, who sat on the edge of the bed, his head in his hands. "He did."

"Thank you, Christoph," said Angus, getting to his feet. "I won't forget you saved my life." He looked at Millie. "I won't forget either of you saved my life. You're both very brave."

As Millie reached into the sack and felt the warmth of feathers against her fingers, she raised her eyebrows at Angus. "Those aren't words I ever thought I'd hear a naked man saying to me," she said. "But you're welcome. You saved mine first."

Christoph shook his head. "It wasn't all bravery on my behalf," he admitted. "When I saw what was going on outside, I ran straight back into the medical centre. I'm ashamed to say I almost didn't help. I listened and watched through the door. Hoping I was dreaming."

"But you did help, even though it was a nightmare," said Millie, prodding Reuben gently as he lay snoring in her palm. She looked at the pale man. "What did you mean about what's going on outside?"

Lifting a set of hospital scrubs from a hook on the

wall, Angus struggled to get into the clothing a few sizes too small for him. He frowned as he spoke. "You should prepare yourself, Millie," he said. "Things are… hectic out there."

"Hectic?" said Millie, prodding her familiar again. "What do you mean, hectic? Where are my father and sister? They must have asked you to come and help me?"

"I've never been one to mince my words," said Angus. "So, I won't start now. Your father's… how can I put it? Not himself. When your sister shouted at me to come in here to help you, she was trying to help your dad."

"What's happened to him? What do you mean, he's not himself?" said Millie. "What's going on out there?"

"The world's gone mad," mumbled Christoph, lying on the bed and pulling the sheet across himself. "Wake me up when it's over."

Then, Reuben wriggled in Millie's hand. "Oh," he said, through a yawn. "Hello. I fell asleep."

"How the hell could you fall asleep?" said Millie, anxiety gripping her as she got to her feet and hurried to the door.

"It's an innate part of the cockatiel I'm in the body of," said Reuben. "Whenever anybody drapes a piece of material over a bird, it tricks us into thinking it's night-time. It's a weakness, I admit, but I had a pleasant forty winks."

"I hope you're wide awake now," said Millie as she

pushed through the door, rushing to whatever hellish nightmare waited for her outside. "I have a feeling that things are about to get weird."

Hurrying after her, the scrubs he wore ready to burst at the seams, Angus spoke. "Prepare yourself," he said. "Get that magic of yours ready. I think you're going to need it."

Chapter 19

Hearing screaming and shouting before she opened the door, Millie prepared herself for what horrors lay waiting on the other side.

A cold blast of air hit her as she stepped outside, pursued by a wave of disbelief as she took in her surroundings.

"I told you it was a bit hectic out here," said Angus, standing barefoot in the snow beside her.

Millie wasn't sure that the word hectic did the circumstances unfolding in Kilgrettin Market Square justice. Hectic would have been pavements full of busy shoppers scurrying home with last-minute purchases, as the shops prepared to close for the last time before Christmas Day. Hectic would have been roads heavy with traffic.

What Millie was looking at was more than hectic.

It was as if a child's worst nightmare was playing out on the pretty, snow-blanketed streets of Kilgrettin.

Everywhere she looked, there were snowmen. Not snowmen that simply stood where they'd been built, waiting for warm weather or a petulant child to destroy them. The snowmen that populated the streets of Kilgrettin were alive.

Some working in groups, and others working alone, the snowmen slid through the snow as if on rails. Their hideous grins contorted beneath their stubby noses, and their pebble eyes glinted like rubies amid their cold, hard features.

Scurrying among the snowmen, pointing at adults and children alike, were hundreds of elves. Screeching commands at the snowmen, they indicated their targets with jabbing fingers. "She's naughty!" shouted one.

"Him next!" yelled another.

As the snowmen obeyed the commands of the tiny dictators, children and adults ran across roads and pavements, attempting to dodge the snowmen as if playing a massive game of tag. Those unfortunate enough to be cornered by the creatures cowered and begged until one of the snowmen reached for them with a gnarly stick arm.

Millie stared in horror as a group of snowmen cornered a young couple, and an elderly man was trapped in a shop doorway by a lone snowman. As the snowman gripped the old man's wrist, his walking stick defence futile, his clothes fell from his body in a heap on the floor. Where the man had stood, now stood a grinning snowman — the flat cap on its head the only indication of who it had been.

Sliding away from the pile of clothes, the newly formed snowman joined the others — heading for a lady who slipped and thudded to the ground as she tried to make her escape.

Moving rapidly towards her, a snowman reached her before she could get to her feet, and within seconds her clothes had joined the others which lay scattered around the square.

Then, booming over the rooftops, came a loud, happy voice. “Ho! Ho! Ho!”

Millie saw him immediately. His sleigh glowing brightly, and his reindeers galloping along a trail of dust which formed before them as they sped past the church tower, Santa cracked the reins with one hand as he waved cheerily with the other. “Merry Christmas!” he bellowed. “When my snowmen have dealt with the naughty children, the rest of us can have a wonderful Christmas together! Ho! Ho! Ho!”

Angus took a few steps forward and reached for a pile of clothes near the gate. He picked up a pair of hospital clogs and forced his feet into the footwear. Then he plucked the white nurse’s jacket from the snow and read from the name tag pinned to the breast pocket. “Jemima,” he said. “She won’t be needing these. They’re a bit small, but they’ll do.”

Then, her eyes raking the panicked crowds, Millie saw her sister standing alongside Maggie. Having placed themselves between a group of people who cowered at the base of the town's Christmas tree, and the hordes of snowmen which tried to reach them, the two witches cast spell after spell at the creatures which closed in on them.

"There's my sister!" said Millie, relieved that Judith had found her magic. She scanned the crowds, looking for the face of her father. "Where's my dad? You said something had happened to him. Did you mean he's one of… those things?"

Angus nodded. "I saw it happen. Your sister tried her best to save him, but there were too many of them. I'm afraid he's one of them now."

"Your father won't like that," observed Reuben, climbing from Millie's pocket and scrambling onto her shoulder. "He doesn't do well in the cold."

"I think that's the least of his worries," said Millie. She ran for the open gate. "We've got to do something!"

"Be careful!" called Angus, as Millie stepped onto the pavement.

Skidding as she changed direction to dodge a snowman wearing a felt-hat adorned with a fake flower, she shouted a reply. "You be careful, too."

As she crossed the road, strewn with the clothing of the newest conscripts to the snowman army, she charged her hand with energy and released a spell aimed at the three snowmen which closed in on a woman and young child they'd cornered. As one of the snowmen reached for her hand, the woman screamed. "Stay away from my child!"

The spell smashed into the attackers, and like pins at a bowling alley, they tumbled left and right as the ball of energy crashed through them. The head of one snowman toppled from its shoulders, the stumpy carrot which had been its nose landing in the snow alongside it.

The second snowman vanished in an explosion of snow, but the third snowman, wearing a bobble hat, began to thaw. Rather than turn to water, the snowman transformed into a mercury like substance as it melted, the metallic liquid spreading through the snow, glistening brightly as it began taking on a shape.

Suddenly, in a mist of sparkling dust, the shimmering shape became flesh, and a naked man lay in the snow. With an expression of horror on his face, he scrambled to his feet and ran away, his scream joining the others which filled the streets.

As Millie sidestepped another snowman, the woman she'd saved grabbed her son and brought him to her chest. "Thank you!" she said. "Whoever you are." Then, dashing through a gap between two approaching snowmen, she followed the naked man, disappearing into an alleyway between two shops.

"At least we know we can help the people who've been turned into snowmen," said Reuben. "But how did you know that would happen? You might have killed that man, rather than saving him."

Running faster, snow crunching beneath her boots

and cold air burning her throat, Millie swallowed. "I didn't," she admitted. "It didn't even cross my mind. I acted instinctively. I was lucky. That man was lucky."

As more snowmen drifted into the square, arriving through alleyways and side streets, the market square rang with shouts and screams. Flying in circles above the square, Santa roared with laughter as he encouraged his Christmas army.

Nearing the Christmas tree, where her sister and Maggie fought off wave after wave of snowmen, Millie called out. "Judith!"

Aiming a stream of red sparks at a trio of snowmen, Judith glanced at Millie. "You made it!" she said, the spell she'd cast turning two snowmen into meltwater, while another spell fizzed at her fingertips.

Reaching the two witches, Millie fired a spell at a snowman that grabbed for her with grasping stick fingers. "Angus saved me," she said, her spell decapitating her attacker.

"Is Angus okay?" asked Maggie, sending a ball of lilac energy into the mob of snowmen, destroying several and transforming one into a woman who clambered to her feet and ran screaming through the crowded ranks of Santa's army.

"He's fine," answered Millie. "He told me what happened to Dad! Where is he?"

"I couldn't save him," said Judith. "There were too many of them. I didn't have my magic until Maggie recharged it for me. Dad went off with a group of snowmen to another part of town. I was forced to retreat."

"They're everywhere," said Maggie. "They're all over town — them and those hideous elves — they're forcing their way into people's homes — nobody's safe!"

"She's the naughtiest of them all!" screeched an elf, riding on the shoulders of a snowman. It pointed at Millie. "Get her! She's the naughtiest child in town. What happened to Krampus is all her fault!"

Several snowmen joined the swarm of attackers surrounding the Christmas tree. As they closed in on the three witches, more elves began barking orders. "Get those three naughty girls! They're trying to stop us! We can't let them ruin Christmas for everybody else!"

"What are we going to do?" shouted Judith, another burst of energy leaving her fingertips. "There's too many of them for us to hold off. It's only a matter of time, and when we've been turned into snowmen, there's nobody else to stop them!"

"It has to be down to Annie," said Maggie. "It's her magic that started everything! She holds the answer. It's her magic that will bring an end to this."

"We left her at home when we went to her barn," said Millie. "She's not in town!"

"Then I think it's about time I did something useful," announced Reuben. "You three girls try and stay safe — I'll go and get Annie!"

As Reuben launched himself into the cold night

air, Millie shouted after him. "Hurry! Tell her that we need her!" She glanced around the market square at the countless people running from elves and snowmen, their screams and shouts drowning out the Christmas music that drifted from the open door of the Kilted Stag. "Tell her the whole town needs her!"

Millie watched Reuben fly into the night until he was hidden by the snowflakes that continued to fall. Then, she watched Santa as he guided his reindeers in large circles around the periphery of the square.

Still chuckling as he went, his laugh seemed to encourage the snowmen and elves, who began moving more urgently in their quest to punish the naughty children of Kilgrettin.

Her eyes had only been on the sky for a few seconds, but those few seconds had allowed one of the smaller snowmen to sneak up on her.

Staring up at her with burning eyes and a twisted smile, the snowman reached for her, its wooden arm making tiny cracking sounds as it moved.

A spell fizzed at her fingertips, but she knew she was too late.

As the splintered fingers touched her hand, Millie sighed as a comforting calm travelled through her. Her thoughts now moving slowly through her mind, serenely instead of frantically, she embraced what was happening.

Then, as she watched her fingers turn to twigs, a loud, high-pitched sound drew her attention. Moving her head slowly to the left, clothes falling from her as she allowed the trivial problems of humanity to melt away, she wondered what the strange girl with blonde hair and blue eyes was doing.

Her mouth wide open, she was emitting an awful screaming sound, and she appeared sad as she said some words which Millie tried to decipher as the last of her clothing fell from her, and her heart turned to ice. “Get off my sister!” the strange girl appeared to be shouting.

Then, as the shouting girl’s words ceased to make sense to her, she watched as a hand of twigs wrapped itself around the screaming girl’s hand, and she became one of them, too.

Chapter 20

With a frigid heart at its core, *it* dragged itself towards the naughty child near the Christmas tree. Her hair as red as Santa's favourite reindeer's nose and her face far too angry for Christmas, the child's hand created sparks, which she used to hurt Santa's helpers.

It knew it was too late for the child, though. There were too many of them now. Their guiding elves pointing and shouting commands at them, the others like *it* moved closer to the last naughty child in that part of town.

This one was particularly naughty, *it* thought. She needed to become one of them as soon as possible, so the nice children of the town could begin having fun.

Changing direction, *it* joined the others as they closed in on the naughty girl with red hair. She wasn't naughty for much longer. Even as she created more of the pretty sparks at her fingertips, damaging some of Santa's helpers, it was too late for her. A long twig finger stroked her wrist and then she was like them.

Satisfied that no more naughty children remained nearby, *it* pulled itself through the snow, the strong instinct within *it* telling *it* to search out more naughty children.

It followed one of the elves which hurried through the snow as it led the army to other naughty children. The ones that remained inside their homes.

As *it* listened to Santa laughing, a shiver of welcoming cold ran through *it.* Santa was happy. He could begin delivering his presents as soon as the last naughty child had become one of them.

There was a lot of naughty children and not many nice children. The good children would have a wonderful Christmas, *it* thought. Santa would share the presents out between them. There'd be so many gifts for each of the good children. What a wonderful Christmas!

Travelling beneath the colourful lights that the humans had strung across the road, *it* followed the others that led the way. So many of them. More of them in the town than there were humans.

It practised using its fingers, preparing them for when *it* caught a naughty child of its own. The magic which Santa had placed in *its* core would work quickly on a naughty child, making it wish it had been nice.

Then, an opportunity to punish a naughty child presented itself. Running from its home, three of the elves pointed at it, trying to get the attention of a snowman.

It responded, shuffling quickly through the snowflakes. The naughty child made loud noises, screaming at the elves, and kicking out at them with his feet.

It gathered pace. This was a really naughty boy. He had to be stopped! *It* reached the naughty boy as he shouted again.

Making claws of its hands, *it* approached the naughty child, his mouth moving again beneath the beard it grew on its chin — not as impressive as Santa's, or of the same colour, it still looked nice.

Looks could be deceiving, though. Although the child looked nice on the outside, *it* was instinctively aware that the child was very naughty on the inside.

It knew why he was naughty, too. *It* didn't know exactly what the words meant, but somehow *it* knew that the naughty boy had told his wife he'd stopped spending something called money on internet gambling sites. Then he'd gone back on his promise and spent lots of money on them. According to the instructions that Santa sent *it* through magic, that was *very* naughty indeed.

Intercepting the naughty child as he reached the bottom of the garden path, *it* blocked his way, and as the three elves pointed and shouted at the naughty child, *it* reached for him with a grasping hand.

The touch of human skin was exhilarating,

and *it* felt a welcome jab of freezing cold in its core as the naughty boy began to change.

When the boy was the same as *it*, *it* continued its journey alongside the other snowmen that trudged through the streets of the town which brimmed with naughty children.

The occasional scream joined Santa's laughter as he flew above them, helping to guide them on their righteous quest.

Then, as *it* enjoyed the cold which gave *it* life, something changed.

It slowed, the others leaving it behind as they trudged forward. *It* tried to match their speed, but something was wrong. Very wrong.

Then, burning. Burning all over *it*. Then colour. Colour rose from its base, rising in tiny lights that twisted around *it*, burning *it* each time they touched its body.

Then, images came to its mind. Terrifying images. *It* saw the girl with blonde hair screaming as a snowman touched her hand. Screaming for the snowman to leave her sister alone. The blonde hair, the blue eyes, *she* knew who it was!

"Judith!" cried Millie, shivering as she lay naked in the snow.

"Millie," squawked Reuben, landing in the snow beside her, dropping what appeared to be a turkey baster alongside him.

Her teeth chattering, Millie stared at the little bird. "What happened? Where am I?"

"You were a snowman, I squirted you with some of the updated eggnog that Annie's made. Now you're not a snowman."

"You saved me," said Millie, a strange memory swirling through her mind. She recalled what she'd done to the poor man who'd been running from his house. She shuddered with shame.

"I didn't save you," said Reuben. "That pendant your father gave you was what saved you."

Millie put a hand to her neck, feeling the jewellery. "It's still there."

"It was around your neck," said Reuben. "It couldn't fall off when you turned into a snowman."

Covering her chest with both arms, Millie looked around. The Christmas tree was only a hundred metres behind her. That was the last place she remembered being. That must be where her clothes were. "Why did the pendant save me?"

Reuben cocked his head. "I'm already aware that we've been referring to all these *snowpeople*, as *snowmen* — so I don't wish to be called any sort of *ist*, or be accused of bigotry… but you snowpeople all look the same. I was lucky enough to spot your pendant. *You* were lucky."

"Thank you," said Millie, the soles of her feet freezing. She stood up and grabbed the turkey baster from the snow. "What's this?"

"Annie's been working on a spell that will reverse the magic she created," said Reuben. "She repeated what she was doing when she turned her husband into Santa. She'd been making magical eggnog when it happened, so she made it again, this time concentrating on reversing her mistake. She's on her way with bottles full of it and lots of these little water squirters. She's got boxes of them for some reason."

"She owns a butcher's shop," said Millie, shivering. "She probably sells them."

"If you say so," said Reuben, "although I'm not sure why a butcher's shop would sell children's toys."

The cold stinging her feet, Millie began running towards the Christmas tree. "Come on. I have to get my clothes. Then we have to help everybody else."

With the army of snowmen leaving the town centre, spreading into the small suburbs of the town, Kilgrettin Market Square was eerily empty. With only the sound of Christmas songs drifting from the door of the Kilted Stag, Millie felt no need to cover herself as she ran towards the Christmas tree.

Panic strangled her as she saw her sister's clothes in a pile, then she recognised the woolly sweater that Maggie had been wearing, alongside a pair of jeans.

She found her own clothes quickly, the birthday jumper which her sister had bought her affording her immediate warmth as she pulled it over her head. Wriggling into her jeans and footwear, she stared along the road as the headlights of a car appeared.

"It's Annie," said Reuben. "She left at the same time I did."

The shout of a man drifted from behind her, and

Millie turned to face the pub. The man shouted again. "Help me! Somebody help me!"

Grasping the turkey baster which dribbled yellow liquid from the tip, Millie hurried towards the pub as the car drew up alongside the tree and Annie stepped out. "Did it work?" she said, her frightened eyes on Reuben.

"It did," said Millie. "Five minutes ago, I was a snowman. Reuben saved me with your eggnog."

"How awful!" said Annie. "Reuben told me what's been happening here. I've been working to reverse my magic since you took me home, but I didn't know it had got this bad in town. I'm so relieved that my eggnog worked."

The man in the pub shouted again, and Millie hurried towards the open door, the turkey baster in her hand. "It's about to get tested again," she said.

She entered the pub to the Christmas sounds of Slade, and looked down as her feet splashed in a puddle of water. Meltwater.

The trail of water led to the bar, and as Millie pushed the door open, she raised the turkey baster like a pistol when she saw what was happening.

Maggie's barman, Francis, stood on the bar, his face as white as the creatures below him which prevented him from climbing down, both of them grasping for his legs as he kicked out at them.

He shouted again, but then as the door closed with a thud behind Millie, he turned in her direction. "Help me!" he yelled.

Ignoring Millie, the snowmen continued in their attempts to transform the barman into one of them. Puddles of water surrounded them, and Millie wondered if eventually, they would melt away into nothing. The dying fire in the hearth was speeding up the process, but even as they slowly turned to water, they still fought to reach the man on the bar.

Aiming the baster, Millie strode towards the first snowman. Unaware of her presence, it continued to grasp for the man. She squirted yellow liquid at it, the stream of eggnog grabbing the snowman's attention as soon as it splashed its body.

It turned to face her, but then its body began losing its form, turning into the same silver liquid she'd witnessed the old man transforming into. She aimed at the other snowman and showered it in a cloud of Annie's magical eggnog. It made one last attempt at reaching the man on the bar but then slumped to the floor, silver fluid flowing from it.

"These are people who were turned into snowmen," explained Millie, turning to Annie, who stood in the doorway looking terrified. "Santa's snowmen just disappear, but humans turn to this silver liquid before regaining their real form."

As Millie turned back to the bar, her heart missed several beats, and she threw herself to the floor alongside the young woman who stared up at her with horrified eyes. "Judith!" she said. "It's you!"

"What happened?" said Judith, suddenly realising she was naked, wrapping her arms around her chest.

"The snowmen got you," said Millie, taking her sister in a fierce hug.

Then, the broad tones of a Scottish accent. "I usually see people like Angus lying on the floor next to my bar after too many whiskies. I never thought I'd be doing it."

"Maggie!" said Annie. "It's you!"

"I thought I'd have a hard job of finding you two," said Millie. "There are hundreds of snowmen out there, they're spreading throughout town looking for people. Luckily, you two came in here, and I heard the barman shouting for help."

Clambering from the bar, the barman stared down at his employer as she got to her feet. "Maggie! You were a snowman!"

Fixing him with a fierce glare, Maggie scowled. "I'd prefer it if you looked the other way until I can get some clothes on, Francis." She winked at Millie as the young man blushed. "I remember knowing that Francis was in here when I was turned into a snowman," she said. "I had vague memories of him hiding behind the bar. I must have come in to get him, and Judith must've followed me in here." She frowned. "How did you save us?"

"It was my eggnog!" said Annie. "We can save everybody, Maggie! I've made some fresh eggnog! It turns snowmen back into people. And if we spray Santa with it, all this will go away."

"I'm not sure you understand how many of them

are out there," said Millie, frowning. "There are hundreds of them. Thousands, maybe."

"I've got plenty of eggnog in the car," said Annie. "And plenty of turkey basters, too."

"That's not the problem," said Millie. "The problem is how we're going to spray all the snowmen and elves with it. We can't just run around town spraying each of them individually. We need a better method. A way of spraying a lot of them at once."

Then, grabbing a tablecloth from a nearby table and wrapping it around herself, Judith pointed towards Millie's chest. "I've got an idea," she said.

Millie gazed down at herself, and then a smile spread across her face. The letters were upside down, but she knew what they said. *It's my birthday, and I'll fly if I want to.*

Chapter 21

As Maggie and Judith wriggled into their clothes, Millie stared along the empty street. "Dad's out there somewhere," she said, looking at Judith as she pulled her coat on. "He's a snowman. I never thought I'd say that."

"I imagine by now everybody I know, and love is a snowman," said Maggie, following Millie's gaze. "My family. My friends. My customers."

Annie stared skyward. "My husband's flying around in a sleigh somewhere. I watched him leaving the barn earlier."

"He's still up there," said Millie. "Controlling his Christmas Army."

A cold wind blew along the street, whipping up tiny tornadoes of snow. Annie pulled her hat down over her ears. "Then let's put a stop to his fun and games," she said. "I want my Clive back. It's

Christmas Day tomorrow, and he always cooks dinner!"

Millie nodded, and striding towards the SUV still parked outside the medical centre, began charging her magic. The last time she'd made the car fly, it had been to save her family. The stakes were just as high now, she told herself, sparks at her fingertips.

She stood staring at the red vehicle, energy fizzing from her hands. Then, with determination and confidence, she aimed a spell at the car, commanding it to permeate every last piece of the SUV.

As Judith reached her side, Millie pushed more magic into the vehicle, relieved when the paintwork began glowing. She looked at her sister. "It's ready."

"I wish I could do that," said Judith.

"The ability is within you," said Millie. "You just need the right circumstances to find it."

"You certainly know your way around a spell," said Maggie, carrying four cola bottles full of eggnog.

"Is it safe?" asked Annie, her coat pockets stuffed with turkey basters. "I didn't know magic could be this powerful!"

"Don't worry," said Judith, opening the passenger door as Millie got into the driver's seat. "This is my sister's magic. It's perfectly safe."

As Reuben took his position on the dashboard, Millie filled a turkey baster from one of Annie's bottles. "Open your windows," she said, turning the key in the ignition, wanting the headlights to work. "I'll fly us above the snowmen and elves. Squirt as many as you can. If we get the chance to squirt Santa, we'll take it — I think that will end this whole nightmare a lot quicker."

Judith held a full turkey baster and smiled at Millie. "Locked and loaded! You have permission to take off!"

Remembering how the spell had worked the day before, Millie squeezed energy from her fingers and told the car what to do.

Annie shrieked as the car rose, gaining height and rocking gently from side to side until the occupants were staring down at the snow-covered rooves of buildings. "Can we get this over with as quickly as possible? I don't like heights." She stared into the night sky. "Neither does Clive! He'd never fly around in that damn sleigh if he weren't Santa!"

Urging the car forward, Millie followed the road below them. It wasn't long before Judith pointed through the windscreen. "There!" she said.

Losing a little altitude, the car swooped lower, and Millie stared in morbid fascination at the long line of snowmen and elves which danced, scurried and dragged themselves through the street. Blending in with the snow, and standing shoulder to shoulder, the snowmen resembled an avalanche that somehow defied physics — requiring no gravity to provide momentum.

Elves rode on the sloping shoulders of snowmen as if they were beasts of war, and people ran from houses, pursued by elves which drove them into the horde, where they quickly assimilated with the avalanche of snowmen.

"Look!" said Maggie. Pointing at the mountains to the east. "Santa!"

"It's Clive!" said Annie. "He's *not* Santa!"

"He's fat, he's wearing a red suit and he looks like he hasn't shaved since nineteen seventy-four," noted Reuben. "I'm sorry, lady, but right now — he's Santa!"

"Then let's get my husband back," said Annie, leaning from her open window, turkey baster ready. "We'll begin by getting rid of his Christmas Army!"

Commanding the car lower, Millie leaned from her window, too. Squeezing the bulb of the turkey baster, she sprayed a cloud of eggnog towards the parade of strange creatures which marched below them.

The momentum of the car and the cold winter wind caused the eggnog to disperse in fine clouds of droplets, which drifted to the floor behind them as they zoomed across the heads of snowmen.

"It's working!" said Maggie, staring through the rear window. "It's working!"

Emptying her turkey baster, Millie sucked up fresh ammunition from the bottle forced into the cup holder. She sprayed another cloud of the magical liquid through the window as the car gained speed.

Reaching the front ranks of the army, Millie turned the SUV in a tight U-turn and told it to hover. She stared at the powerful effects the eggnog had produced. Snowmen crumbled, elves vanished in little puffs of magic dust, and humans lay naked in the snow as they transformed to their usual selves.

"Make another pass!" said Reuben. "Let's eggnog those bastards back to hell!"

Her turkey baster loaded, Millie commanded the car forward. It accelerated quickly, knocking Reuben from the dashboard.

The bird scrambled to his feet on Millie's lap, and then looked up at his witch. "I'm going to find your father," he said. "When he's transformed back into a human by the eggnog, he's going to be very perturbed about lying naked in the snow. He's a very private gentleman. I'll put his mind at rest by telling him what's happened!"

As the little bird launched himself through the open window into the cold wind, Millie yelled after him. "Be careful!"

Flying low across the army, the car's shadow only feet beneath them, the four witches opened fire with eggnog, destroying more elves and snowmen.

Then, Judith squealed. "Watch out!"

Millie looked up, and with seconds to spare, banked sharply to the left, narrowly missing the hooves of Santa's reindeer as they hurtled towards the car.

"Ho! Ho! Ho!" bellowed Santa. "What do you think you naughty children are doing? I can't allow you to do that! I need my snowmen and elves!"

As the car straightened out, Judith looked over her shoulder. "Oh, no! He's undoing the damage we did!"

Turning the car to face the sleigh, Millie stared at the scene beneath her. Flying above his army, Santa continued to laugh as an elf sat atop the pile of presents in the rear of the sleigh, sprinkling magical dust from a sack.

The dust fell like a shattered rainbow, bringing life to the snow wherever it landed. Forming quickly, snowmen appeared, the severed twig arms from destroyed snowmen finding new bodies.

Elves wriggled as they popped into existence — leaping upon snowmen and guiding them through the streets.

Naked people ran amongst the carnage, some of them making it into houses, but most of them being caught by snowmen, their transformation into human having been disappointingly brief.

Emptying the contents of her baster, Millie stared in frustration. "It had no effect!" she said, watching as the eggnog landed harmlessly among the army. "Santa's dust is too powerful."

"Then we have to take Santa out," said Annie. "This all began when Clive turned into him. When he becomes Clive again, I have a feeling this nightmare will be over."

"Oh no," said Judith, glancing at the dashboard. "It's eleven-forty. You heard what he said in the barn, Millie. If he's still here at midnight, he'll be here forever."

"Okay," said Millie, aiming the car at Santa's sleigh. "Prepare to spray him. I'll get as near as I can. We have twenty minutes in which to save this town and its people." She looked at her sister. "Our father, too."

As the car sped towards the sleigh, Santa cracked the reins he held in his gloved hands. The red nose of the leading reindeer glowed brightly as the sleigh gained speed, and Millie panicked, as with remarkable speed, the sleigh gained height and hurtled towards them on a collision course.

"Go lower!" yelled Judith, ducking in her seat. "He's going to hit us!"

Millie hadn't needed telling. The boom of her heartbeat thumping in her ears, the command had already been given. The car dropped quickly, but not fast enough. With a sickening crack, Rudolph's heavy hooves smashed into the windscreen, sending spider-webs of cracks through the glass.

As the herd thundered above them, the hooves of the other reindeers hammered the sheet metal roof, one of them penetrating the glass of the sunroof, narrowly missing Millie's head.

Then the sleigh hit. The thick oak runners smashed into the vehicle, shaking it violently, sending it tumbling towards the ground.

"Watch out!" yelled Maggie. "We're going to crash!"

Closing her eyes, Millie forced energy from her chest, commanding the car to react. Spiralling out of control, the ground approaching quickly, the car failed to respond.

She tried again, panic in her throat. Nobody would survive the impact if the car crashed at this speed. The four people in the car would be dead, and many of the poor people who ran terrified from snowmen and elves would die as the car crashed among them.

Shaking her head, Millie shouted. "You're not going to ruin my birthday, Santa!" The muscles in her arms cramped painfully as she forced more energy through them. Clenching her teeth, she flooded the vehicle with energised magic, commanding it to aim for the stars.

This time, the car responded, and as the wheels skimmed the heads of snowmen, it changed direction, gaining height.

"That was too close!" said Annie, her voice cracking.

"He's coming back!" said Maggie. "He's going to ram us again!"

With seconds to spare, Millie forced the car to the right, the reindeer's hooves barely missing the cracked windscreen as Santa attempted to knock them from the skies.

Splintered glass tumbled into the car as a hoof found the already compromised sunroof, shattering it into thousands of pieces.

"Ho! Ho! Ho!" came Santa's haunting laugh as the sleigh whizzed past, inches above them.

"Damn you, Saint Nicholas," shouted Maggie. "Watch where you're going."

"Look," said Judith, pointing at the ground. "There are more snowmen. There must be thousands of them."

As Millie guided the car into a turning loop, she stared at the ground in dismay. With Santa's elf liberally sprinkling dust across the snowy landscape, snowmen rose in their hundreds, like zombies rising from the dead.

Frustrated, she guided the car towards the bright red sleigh which flew low over the rooves of houses.

"We have to get him," said Judith.

"He thinks the same about us," noted Maggie, pointing through the cracked windscreen. "Look! He's coming for us again!"

With Rudolph's bright nose leading the way, the reindeers and heavy sleigh sped towards them. Behind the reins, Santa bellowed with laughter, his laugh ricocheting off the mountains that surrounded the town, amplifying it above all other sounds.

The cold wind whipping through the sunroof and open windows, Millie glanced upwards. Snowflakes drifted into the car, and then Millie looked at Judith.

She took her sister's hand as Santa bore down on them. "You have to fly the car," she said. "I've got an idea."

"No," said Judith, shaking her head vigorously. "I can't make the car fly!"

Sending energy from her hand to her sister's,

Millie nodded. "You can," she said. "You just have to believe in yourself. Just like Santa and his army have come to life because of people's beliefs, your magic will respond in the same way. Whatever you believe your magic can do, it will do. You just have to want it enough."

Then, she pushed herself into a crouching position on her seat, her hair whipped by the wind as she moved her head to the sunroof. "I'm passing over control of the car to you, Judith. You have to get me close enough to Santa. We're only going to stop him if one of us can get near him — and he doesn't look like he's going to land any time soon."

No," snapped Judith. "I can't fly this car, and you're not going to attempt a leap from a flying car onto a sleigh being dragged by reindeers. You'll kill yourself, Millie, and I'll kill the rest of us when I crash the car. This is not an action film!"

"He's coming again!" shouted Annie.

Bearing down on them, Santa cracked the reins as the sleigh hurtled out of a tight turn. Rudolph's nose glowed brighter, and targeting the car, galloped at them like a laser-guided missile.

Millie smiled at her sister. "You might not believe in yourself, but I do. I've put a little of my car flying spell into your hand. Just concentrate on the way it works, and you'll be fine."

As Millie pulled herself through the sunroof, freezing wind attacked her face. With snowflakes blinding her, she pulled first one leg, and then the other onto the roof of the car, her hands gripping the roof bars.

"I won't be able to fly this thing," warned Judith. "Please get back in. There has to be another way to get to him!"

As the grunting of reindeers approached, and Santa's smiling face stared into hers, Millie gave the car one last command.

Moving quickly, the car rose higher than Santa and his reindeers, and as the whites of Rudolph's eyes became visible, Millie prepared to leap. "You've got this, Judith!" she yelled, her thighs tensed as she prepared to release her tight grip on the roof bars.

"I can't fly this thing!" shouted Judith. "Please get back in here!"

There was no going back. Thrusting herself from the car roof, she aimed at the back of the nearest reindeer. As her fingers released the roof bars, and her body became airborne, she shouted. "You are flying it! You've been flying it for the last ten seconds!"

With a strong crosswind buffeting her, and the ground fatally distant beneath her, Millie put her faith in fate as she travelled through empty air, praying she had timed her jump well.

Chapter 22

Her breath leaving her in a painful whoosh, and the hard-muscled back of a reindeer writhing beneath her as it galloped through the cold air, Millie slammed into the flying herd.

Snowflakes zipped through the air, and the hot, unpleasant breath of a reindeer warmed her face as it grunted its displeasure with a loud huff. She held on tightly to the leather harness of the reindeer as the beast bucked and writhed beneath her.

Then the realisation of the situation she'd placed herself in dawned on her. She'd been reckless. Judith had been correct. She'd watched too many action films.

She glanced towards the moonlit ground and managed a smile as she watched her father's SUV glowing bright red as it made a clean landing in the town square. Judith needed more confidence in her magic. That was all. And when this was over, Millie would help her gain it.

"Get off my reindeers!" roared Santa. "You are such a naughty child."

Her body bouncing as the beast below her gathered speed, Millie lifted her head. "You shouldn't be here," she yelled, the wind carrying her words. "You're not real."

Checking the baster was still in her pocket, she took a deep breath and dragged herself along the back of the reindeer she'd landed on, the velvet antlers of the animal she crawled towards brandished menacingly as she neared it.

Then, Santa cracked the reins, and the reindeers responded, lurching forward with frightening speed, their breath loud and their hooves rumbling on the invisible road beneath them. "Ay-up, boys and girls," he shouted. "Ay-up!"

As Santa yelled his command, the leading reindeers lifted their heads and shot skyward. As the sleigh flew vertically, Millie tumbled. Her fingers lost their grip on the thin leather of the harness, and her breath left her as she thudded into the solid shoulder blade of a galloping reindeer.

An antler grazing her cheek, she twisted her head to avoid being impaled on the next set that awaited her.

Grasping for anything that would break her fall, her hand found a thick leather strap placed around the chest of one of the beasts. Her legs swinging outward with fierce momentum, she barely held on as Santa gave the reindeers another order. As the animals swiftly changed direction, the leather dug into Millie's fingers as her legs trailed behind her in empty air.

"Get her off my sleigh, little Jimmy," yelled Santa.

Managing to get one leg over the back of the reindeer which she held onto for dear life, Millie glanced at the sleigh. The little elf who'd been sprinkling magic dust was bounding towards her, leaping from the front of the sleigh onto the back of a reindeer.

As if not controlled by the same forces of gravity as Millie was, he hopped quickly from reindeer to reindeer until he stood next to Millie's head.

With a grin that would have been cute in any other circumstance, he aimed a pointed boot at her face. "Get off Santa's sleigh," he ordered. Then, he swung his foot.

The elf may have been small, but the tip of his boot was hard. Millie let out a shriek as her cheekbone took the brunt of the blow, pain spreading across her face. The elf aimed another kick, this time slamming into her chin, her jaw crunching as her teeth closed on her tongue.

She let out a yell of pain and instinctively moved a hand towards her face, quickly realising her mistake, grasping for the reindeer's harness once more.

As the elf hopped from foot to foot alongside her, he let out a high-pitched laugh and prepared to kick her once more. "This time I'm going to put some real power behind it!" he boasted.

Then, another voice arrived on the wind. "You little folk are so bloody annoying," came Reuben's angry squawk.

The elf's eyes widened, and he lifted his hands as a blur of feathers slammed into him. Then he was gone, his arm in Reuben's beak and his tiny legs waggling beneath him as he begged to be released. "Let me go! Let me go!"

"Are you sure?" squawked Reuben, his words muffled by the arm in his mouth.

"No!" squeaked the elf, as Reuben carried him into the darkness. "Hold on to me! I'm too small to die! I have my whole Christmas ahead of me!"

As Reuben and the elf vanished into snowflakes and darkness, Millie's familiar called out again. "I found your father! And Angus! They were both angry and naked, and your father was ashamed, but they're okay now!"

A reindeer huffed as Santa urged the herd on, and Millie, her face stinging, secured her grip on the harness.

Ignoring the sting in her cheek, she began tugging herself inch by inch towards the sleigh. Dragging her body across the bouncing, muscled bodies of the animals, and dodging their antlers, she grunted as large bones and solid muscle slammed into her body.

As she neared the sleigh, Santa cracked the reins

again, urging the reindeers forward. "Why are you trying to ruin Christmas?" he bellowed.

Her hand finding the smooth wood of the sleigh, she held on tight as she removed the turkey baster from her pocket. She looked at Santa. "I'm trying to have a Christmas!" she yelled. "My first Christmas with a father! You are not going to spoil it for me!"

Aiming the tip of the baster at the bearded face, Millie squeezed the liquid-filled bulb. Eggnog, carried by the wind, splattered the driver of the sleigh, colourful dust beginning to rise from him as the first drop of magical liquid touched the rosy skin of his cheek.

As Santa dropped the reins, lifting both hands to his face and falling backwards into the pile of presents, Millie pulled herself forward as the reindeer bolted in panic.

Gathering speed, the frightened animals headed for the church tower that rose from the centre of Kilgrettin, its thick stone walls and illuminated clock face a fearsome obstacle which would smash the sleigh to pieces.

Santa writhed among the presents as Millie took the reins. She looked ahead, searching her memory for the names she knew must be there.

She recalled the easiest one first. The most obvious one. "Rudolph!" she yelled. Then the others came, riding on happy memories of childhood Christmases. "Dasher, Dancer, Prancer, Vixen, Comet, Cupid, Donner and Blitzen — calm down!"

She pulled at the reins, not sure how to communicate her wishes to the animals. She wanted them to veer left, but the reindeers continued on their collision course with the tower. She spoke to them again. "Turn left! Please!"

Then, as the church tower loomed, the big hand a hair's breadth from indicating midnight, Santa spoke from behind her. "Ay up," he yelled. "Ay up, girls and boys! Take us down now, take us down now!"

The reindeers responded immediately, and the church tower zoomed past them, the sleigh missing it by a few short inches.

As the sleigh neared the ground, the reindeer slowing to a trot as their breath rose in thick clouds, Santa spoke again, this time his voice softer. "I just wanted the children to have a wonderful Christmas."

Millie turned to look at him, the sleigh itself now turning to dust. He was different. His beard was shorter, his nose smaller and his eyes gentler. He gave a warm smile. "Have a very merry Christmas, Millie Thorn!" he mumbled, as the last of his beard retreated into his chin, and the red fur-lined suit he wore transformed into a white jacket and a striped apron.

No sooner had Santa become Clive, than the sleigh began evaporating around them. As Rudolph's hoof touched the snow, he disintegrated too, vanishing in a cloud of rainbow dust.

As each of the reindeers landed, they turned to

dust too, the sound of their heavy breathing fading on the wind.

Then, as if Millie had imagined the whole thing, she sat in a pile of snow with a sore face and a confused man staring at her.

He gave her a puzzled look, and then his eyes fell to her hand. "Is that one of my turkey basters?" he asked.

Chapter 23

"Merry Christmas!" said Judith, shaking Millie's shoulder. "It's time to get up! Dad's excited about opening his presents!"

Her head groggy, Millie prised her eyes open. Was it really time to get up? It seemed like only five minutes ago that she'd crawled into bed after ensuring the town was free of Christmas monsters and that the residents were as calm as could be expected after the ordeal they'd been through.

She gazed up at her sister, wiping sleep from her eyes. "What time is it?"

"Seven o'clock," said Judith. "You've had four hours sleep. That's plenty. Come on, we didn't get to celebrate your birthday properly — let's make sure that Christmas Day is a good one." She put a hand to her sister's face. "Any pain?"

Opening and closing her jaw, Millie shook her

head. "No," she said. "You cast a perfect healing spell last night."

Judith beamed. "Dad says the same. Krampus broke two of his ribs, tore his thigh muscle and gave him a pounding headache." She gave a mischievous wink. "After I laid my healing hands on him, he says he's never felt better!"

"You're a great witch," said Millie. "I've always said that." She looked up into her sister's blue eyes. "You even flew a car last night."

Judith closed her eyes and drew in a breath. She stared at her sister. "Never do that again," she said. "I thought I was going to kill Maggie and Annie. And myself, of course."

"But you didn't," said Millie. "And I didn't jump from the car until I was sure you had control. I knew you could do it. You should be proud. You made a car fly!"

"I wouldn't go that far," said Judith. "I aimed the car at the ground and landed it. There wasn't much flying involved. Anyway… it's time to get up. Come on!"

"Okay," said Millie. "Give me a minute. Let me wash the sleep out of my eyes at least."

After a quick wash, Millie grabbed some jeans and a jumper from the pile of freshly laundered clothes which now smelled of spring blossom instead of Buttered Pecan ice-cream.

Yawning as she plodded from her bedroom into the living area, which smelled of bacon and pancakes, she smiled at her sister and father. "Merry Christmas!" she said, knocking the last sleep-induced cobweb from her mind.

"Merry Christmas, Millie," squawked Reuben.

Glancing at the branch of the Christmas tree on which Reuben was perched, Millie smiled. "You've brought Robin into the cabin?" she asked, peering at the little bird with the red plumage, feasting on a slice of apple.

"Christmas is when everybody comes together!" said Reuben. "I didn't like to think of him being out there in the cold all day. Alone."

"Breakfast?" asked Sergeant Spencer. "I've made sausages, pancakes and bacon."

"Presents first!" said Judith impatiently.

Her father grinned. "Presents first."

Huddled around the Christmas tree, the small family opened the few gifts they'd brought with them from Spellbinder Bay.

Millie opened the Triumph Spitfire Hayne's Manual which Judith had bought her, grinning at her sister. "Perfect," she said.

"I don't expect you to repair your own car," said Judith. "I thought it would be interesting to look through."

Millie laughed. "I'll have a go at repairing the leaking radiator," she said. "You know me, I'll try anything!"

"Laphroaig Ten-year Cask Strength!" said Sergeant Spencer, unwrapping his gift. "This is proper whiskey! You shouldn't have, girls. This couldn't have been cheap."

Having learned that her father ignored the fact that she'd inherited a vast amount of wealth from the bloodline of witches she came from, instead insisting that he enjoyed helping both his daughters financially, Millie leaned towards him and pecked him on the cheek. "You're worth it," she said.

"You are, Dad," said Judith, opening a gift containing her favourite perfume, the one that made her smell like summer, even in the depths of winter.

When all the gifts had been opened, Millie helped her father toss the discarded wrapping paper onto the log fire. The flames consumed it quickly, turning the ink it was printed with into little sparkles of colour. "Do you think everything is okay in town?" she said.

"Of course," said Judith. "You smashed Santa last night! You should have seen the action from ground level — it was like watching a film. You were amazing! Like a superhero!"

"Girls," said Sergeant Spencer. "I already asked Judith before you came in, Millie — I'd like to try and forget about yesterday, for at least a little while. It's not a day I want to dwell on."

"Do you mean the part where you were hobbling along Market Street, completely naked, being chased by snowmen, and with a curious elf trying to grab your devil's noodle?" asked Reuben. "That was quite a sight. I don't think I'd ever get over it, either, if I were you. I'd never live it down."

"That was part of it, Reuben," said Sergeant Spencer, his cheeks reddening. "But the fact that Krampus nearly killed us, we were all turned into snowmen, and Millie risked her life battling Santa as he flew his sleigh, all come into it, too. I don't really want to speak about any of it. At least for today. Let's just enjoy our first Christmas as a family."

"Hear, hear," said Millie, smiling at her father as he added a log to the fire. "No more talk of yesterday." She looked up at Reuben, who passed the robin a piece of fudge from the box balanced on the tree alongside him. "I see you like your present."

Sticky fudge preventing him from fully opening his beak, Reuben nodded, mumbling as he spoke. "My favourite. You know me so well, Millie Thorn."

The fire crackled as Sergeant Spencer rearranged the logs with a poker, the sweet scent of burning pine mingling with the salty aroma of bacon.

He placed the poker back in the brass bucket next to the fireplace and opened a drawer in a small cupboard alongside an armchair. "There's another present for you," he said. "I was asked to give it to you this morning."

"Asked?" said Millie, reaching for the neatly wrapped package that Sergeant Spencer handed her. "Who asked you?"

"I did, Millie," said a soft voice from behind her. "Merry Christmas, darling!"

Millie turned quickly. "Mum!" she said, clutching the package in one hand as she rushed at the ghost.

"Hello, Josephine," said Sergeant Spencer. "How did you get here? You told me there wouldn't be enough magic in Kilgrettin for you to be able to make an appearance."

As Millie reached the apparition, she stared into her mother's kind face as the air crackled behind her, and another voice spoke. "She travelled with me."

Turning to face the familiar voice, Millie stared at the short man in the colourful waistcoat and the little circular glasses. Henry Pinkerton stared back, a frown furrowing his brow.

Millie jumped as Edna Brockett appeared next to him, a loud popping sound accompanying her arrival.

The elderly witch, dressed as neatly as usual, gazed around the cabin. "Oh," she said, unbuttoning her floral cardigan. "It's lovely and warm in here. And look what you've done with the decorations! I'm so glad you appear to like my cabin! Merry Christmas to you all!"

"We love it," said Judith, with a worried smile. "And merry Christmas to you, too, but what are you doing here?"

Clearing his throat, a hand on each of his waistcoat lapels, Henry Pinkerton peered over his little round glasses as he began pacing in front of the fireplace.

He shook his head and then frowned. "I did not expect to be travelling along waves of energy on Christmas Day," he announced. "I'm sure Edna had better things to do, too. Josephine asked to come along, so I'm sure she's thrilled to be here."

The hairs on Millie's forearms stood on end as her mother's ghostly hand moved across her. Then her mother spoke. "I'm delighted to be here, Henry. Thank you for allowing me to piggyback."

"It was a pleasure to transport you, Josephine," smiled Henry. "I'm always happy to help."

"Henry," said Sergeant Spencer, gazing down at the short man. "What are you doing here?"

"As I said," continued Henry. "I did not expect to be here this morning. I expected to be sipping aged brandy in the library of Spellbinder Hall, but then, as I finished breakfast and prepared for a relaxing day, I foolishly allowed myself to speculate on how Millie Thorn and her wonderful family were enjoying their time away in Edna Brockett's log cabin.

"When I did, the tendrils of energy which connect me to the world of magic lit up brighter than the Christmas tree that Florence had decorated and placed in the corner of the library. When I examined the signals, I was quite shocked to discover what has been happening in this tiny town over the last two days. I was especially shocked to discover what happened here last night. Some potent magic was used here yesterday. Very powerful, indeed."

"Hold on, Henry," said Sergeant Spencer. "It wasn't the girl's fault. It was another witch who caused all the problems."

Henry waved a dismissive hand. "Oh," he said.

"Don't worry. I know what happened. I know about Annie and Clive." He looked at Millie. "I also know that you broke magical protocol by making your car fly on the journey here."

"She saved our lives," protested Judith. "We'd gone over the edge of a cliff!"

"I know that," said Henry. "And I'm certainly not suggesting that Millie shouldn't have used magic in those circumstances. What she should have done, though, is flown you to the nearest place of safety. Not go joyriding above Scotland, enjoying the views."

"I was caught up in the moment," said Millie. "I'm sorry."

"No harm was done," said Henry. "Anyway, that little creative use of magic pales into insignificance compared to what happened in Kilgrettin last night."

"Is everybody in town safe?" asked Edna. "I haven't been here for so long; I'd hate to think that somebody had been hurt."

"Everybody's okay," said Millie. "We saw to that. One man had taken a terrible beating, but because the damage was done by a magical creature, Judith and I were able to heal him quite easily. He's fine now. He's a strong man."

"Good," said Henry. "My powers are limited to sensing when paranormal people have been hurt, not humans. The news that nobody was injured is welcome. All that needs to be done now is for me to wipe the memories of the Kilgrettin residents. I've already cast a spell which has wiped mobile phones and cameras of last night's escapade. That spell is working as we speak, but the memory cleansing spell is going to take a little more work. Edna and I are going to work on it here in the cabin. We hope to have it prepared within an hour or two."

"I'm sorry we're intruding on Christmas Day," said Edna.

"It's your cabin," said Sergeant Spencer. "You're entitled to be here."

"It may be my cabin," said Edna. "But I loaned it to you. I would never have considered infringing upon your time here had it not been so important."

Frustration on his face, Sergeant Spencer shrugged. "We may as well have breakfast. There's plenty to go around."

As Henry and Edna leaned over the cauldron which Edna had located in the cupboard next to the bathroom, Millie sat alongside her mother, who shimmered and flickered in the tartan armchair, the red and black pattern visible through her torso and face. "You got me a present?" she said, the package in her hand.

"Your father and sister helped me, of course," said her mother. "We worked together. I wasn't sure whether to ask your father to give it to you on your birthday, or today. Considering what happened yesterday, I think I made the right choice by choosing today."

Stuffing half a sausage into his mouth, Sergeant Spencer nodded, ketchup on his top lip. "It was the right choice. I enjoyed helping you, Josephine. It reminded me of the time I spent with you when you were alive."

Her lips curling into a smile, Millie's mother looked into the fire. "We did have some good times." She looked at Millie. "Are you going to open it?"

Nodding, Millie plucked at the ribbon tied neatly around the package. Then she peeled a corner open and unfolded the paper, revealing a hardback book with a leather cover. She ran a finger over the gold lettering. "*Where I came from*," she read, licking her lips. She looked at her mother. "What is it?"

"Photographs, darling," said her mother. "Photographs you won't have seen. Some of me, some of your father and sister, and some of us together, before I became pregnant and ran away."

"I'd never seen them either," said Judith. "Dad had kept them in the back of a wardrobe. It's been a revelation to me, too. I have vague memories of your mother from when I was little, Millie, but the photos didn't bring back any recollections."

"You were very young when you and your father moved to the bay, Judith," said Josephine. "And you were both adjusting to life within a paranormal community. You were kept very busy for such a young girl. I'm sure your memories are very muddled."

Millie began prising the cover of the book open, pausing when her mother spoke. "In some of those photographs, I'm pregnant with you. But, of course, your father never knew." She flickered and then sighed. "And we all know why."

"Not today, Josephine," said Sergeant Spencer, gently. "Nobody blames you. We know you ran away because you didn't want a child growing up around magic you considered dangerous."

"It's in the past, Mum," said Millie, reaching for her mother's hand, her fingers tingling as they passed through the apparition. "It doesn't matter. Dad knows about me now, and I know about Dad."

"And I'm happy you have your father," replied her mother. "I'm glad he's here to look after you. All those years you spent without a parent after I died must have been awful for you." She gazed around the room, smiling as her eyes landed on the Christmas tree. "Especially at this time of year."

"Christmas was tough without a parent when I was growing up," admitted Millie. "But I had Aunty Hannah, and even though she isn't blood, she and her whole family treated me like I was one of them. But look around — this is the best Christmas I could have asked for. A Christmas Day with two parents." She reached for Judith and took her hand. "And a sister, of course."

Wiping a finger beneath his eye, Sergeant Spencer made a strange noise in his throat and then stood up. "Then let's stop focusing on the past and enjoy the present! I've got an appointment with a turkey and an oven. And I've got a very expensive bottle of whiskey to open while I'm doing it, thanks to my beautiful daughters."

"He always liked his whiskey," whispered Millie's mother, her lips close to her daughter's ear.

Gently, Millie opened the book. On the first crisp white page was mounted a single photograph. The colour fading, it showed Millie's mother standing alongside her father, and at their feet, holding a doll with flowing blonde hair, sat a little girl. *Judith.*

Moving her head closer to Millie's, her mother placed a shimmering finger on the photograph. "You're in that picture, darling," she said. "You may have been very tiny, but you're there, growing inside me."

A tear warmed her cheek, and Millie ran a finger across the picture, her fingernail remaining on her mother's slim belly for a few moments. "It's lovely," she said.

The next picture had been taken on Spellbinder Bay beach. Judith, and Millie's mother, sat next to each other, each of them clutching a half-eaten sandwich, happy smiles on their faces.

"They were good times," said Millie's mother.

"I couldn't help overhearing," said Edna, approaching the fireplace. "I think it's a wonderful gift to have given your daughter, Josephine." She looked at Millie. "Is there room for another photograph in there?"

Flicking to the back of the book, Millie nodded. "There's a page free."

Turning her hand palm up, Edna closed her eyes, mumbled something under her breath, and in a puff of smoke, an old-fashioned camera appeared in her hand. She looked towards the kitchen. "Sergeant Spencer, get over here. And tidy that hair up. It's time to fill the last page of Millie's book."

Chapter 24

Having developed the photograph with a click of her fingers, Edna looked on as Millie carefully inserted the picture into the book, placing the protective sheet over it. With the pen her father handed her, she wrote beneath it in her neatest handwriting. *Christmas 2019. All I ever wanted.*

Reuben peered at the photograph from Millie's shoulder, Robin watching from the arm of the chair she sat in. "The camera loves me," he announced. "And thank you for allowing Robin to join us. It will give me something to remember him by when we go home."

"Of course," said Millie. "If you love him, we love him, too."

Striding purposefully from the kitchen, Henry clapped his hands, startling Robin, who fluttered back to the safety of the Christmas tree.

"Have some respect, Henry Pinkerton!" scolded

Reuben, landing on a branch alongside his friend. "You scared him!"

"I apologise," said Henry. "But I have news. He held up a tiny bottle, the contents of which glowed orange. "The spell is prepared. The only thing left to do is venture into Kilgrettin and cast it. After a night's sleep, the townsfolk will awake with all recollections of any paranormal occurrences having been removed. We shall leave for town immediately."

He paused and looked towards the window. "Can you hear an engine? Is somebody here?"

Sergeant Spencer strode to the window and peered outside. "It's Angus," he said. "In his tractor. He's towing a car. Maggie's with him."

Edna put a hand on Henry's arm. "Angus is a werewolf. Maggie's a witch. They're like us. They're good people."

Henry nodded and straightened his tie. "Very well," he said.

As the tractor pulled up outside the cabin and the engine rattled to a stop, Sergeant Spencer opened the door as Angus and Maggie strode towards the cabin.

"Merry Christmas!" yelled Angus, with a wave of his hand. "I hope you've all recovered after last night's excitement. I know I barely have."

"Happy Christmas," echoed Maggie.

Returning the greeting, Sergeant Spencer stood aside as they entered the cabin, knocking snow from their boots.

Angus nodded towards the tractor. "I brought you

a car to use until yours is repaired, it'll take a week or so to get fixed. Those reindeer wrecked it!"

As Maggie looked around the cabin, her eyes lit up. "Edna!" she said, hurrying to the elderly lady standing beside the fireplace. "I didn't think I'd ever see you again! Where have you been?"

Returning Maggie's hug, Edna placed a hand on each of her arms. "I've left it far too long, I'm sorry. I've been busy in Spellbinder Bay. I won't leave it this long again."

Angus pointed towards the kitchen. "Pancakes? May I?"

"Help yourself," said Sergeant Spencer.

Removing a glove, Angus rolled a pancake into a cylindrical shape and took a large bite. His eyes widened, and he took another bite. "Wow," he said between chews. "That's good, What's in it?"

With a grin, the policeman shrugged. "Vanilla, sugar and whatnot."

"Whatnot? What's that?" asked Angus.

"It means he's forgotten what he put in them," said Judith.

"I made them by taste," said Sergeant Spencer. "But I think I recall adding cinnamon to the batter."

Popping the last piece of pancake into his mouth, Angus stared at the armchair near the fireplace. "A ghost?" he said, peering at Millie's mother. "We don't see many of those around here. They keep themselves hidden!"

"Angus," said Millie. "Meet my mother. Josephine."

"It's a pleasure to meet you, madam," said Angus. He gave Millie a subdued smile and dipped his chin. "I'm sorry for your loss."

"I'm sitting right here," said Josephine. She gave a gentle laugh and smiled at the werewolf. "I'm not lost!"

Angus grinned. "I've never been in a situation like this before. It's hard to know what to say."

When all the introductions had been made, Angus lowered his gaze to Henry Pinkerton. "How did you get here? The roads are blocked." Then, he smiled. "Flying car?" he asked with a wink.

"My mode of transport is a little more subtle than that," replied Henry.

"Henry travels along strands of energy," said Judith. "And he can bring people with him."

"Why did you come today, Edna?" asked Maggie. "To spend Christmas here?"

"Not quite," said Edna. "We came because of what happened last night."

"We're here to make sure the existence of people like us remains a secret in this town," said Henry. "I'm going to ensure that the paranormal community is safe. I have a spell which will wipe the memories of every non-paranormal person in Kilgrettin. No harm will come to them, but their memories of yesterday's events will be removed."

"But we will be safe," protested Angus. "You don't

have to do that. The people in this town are good people. Even one that I thought was bad has turned out to be good. You don't need to wipe their memories. They've already accepted us."

Removing his glasses, Henry polished the lenses on his shirt sleeve. Reflections of the fire twinkled in them as he replaced them on his face. "I can't allow that," he said. "You only have to study the history books to learn what happens when folk discover people like us are among them. Imagine what would happen if the existence of witches, vampires, ghosts, and people like you, Angus, were discovered. Humanity would hunt us down. Maybe they wouldn't destroy us — but life would be awful for us all, both paranormal and human."

"But Kilgrettin isn't *all* of humanity," said Maggie. "It's less than a thousand people bonded by isolation and long family traditions. The people in this town are strong. And since last night, more paranormal people have made themselves known — people even I didn't know were paranormal. People have been emboldened to step out of the shadows."

"People *none* of us knew were paranormal," added Angus. "Seeing what happened yesterday gave them the courage to be themselves."

"The people aren't scared of us," said Maggie. "In fact, you should come to town. That's why we're here — we came to get the girls and their father. Reuben too, of course. But you should all come — you'll enjoy it." She smiled at Henry. "You might change your mind about wiping people's memories."

"We were about to leave for town," said Henry. "To cast the spell. I shall, of course, have an open mind... but I *will* be casting the spell. I'm afraid it's my duty as one of the protectors of our community."

Angus frowned. "At least make that decision on a full stomach." He strode towards the door, putting his gloves on. "Come on. There's a feast awaiting us."

Chapter 25

Kilgrettin was a completely different place than it had been the night before, and Millie stared in fascination at the spectacle unfolding in the little town square.

Replacing the evil snowmen that had roamed the streets on Christmas Eve, were more traditional variants, their grins friendly and mischievous, rather than callous and menacing.

Children dragged their friends through the snow on toboggans, their breath curling into the cold air, and others threw snowballs at one another, laughing when they hit a bullseye.

Christmas songs drifted from the Kilted Stag, joined by the malty aroma of beer, which did well to make itself known through the mouth-watering smells rising from the most astonishing addition to Kilgrettin Market Square.

"How on earth did they do that?" said Judith, stepping out of the little car Angus had loaned them.

Henry stood alongside her, licking his lips as he took in the sight of the huge feast. "Magic," he said. "And lots of it. I feel it everywhere. I shouldn't allow this."

"But you will, won't you?" said Edna, smelling the air. "You can cast your spell after we've eaten. It appears to me that non-paranormal people and people like us are getting on just fine together. Don't ruin it for them, Henry. Let them have their Christmas Day."

"It's only just midday," said Henry, plucking his pocket watch from his breast pocket. "It's a little early for Christmas dinner."

"Then don't eat yet," suggested Maggie. "There will be food here all day. The witches will see to that."

As a young boy ran past Millie, giggling as his friend threw a snowball at his back, his eyes widened and he came to a halt, a small snowdrift forming at his feet. He gazed up at Millie, awe in his eyes. "Wow!" he said. "It's you! The Santa Slayer!"

"The what?" said Millie, bemused.

It was too late. The boy was moving at speed towards the crowd of people near the Christmas tree, his red wellies sinking in the snow. "She's here!" he yelled. "The Santa Slayer's here!"

As people turned to look at her, Millie glanced at Angus. "What's happening?" she said.

"That's what the kids are calling you. You're a

hero, Millie. Lots of people watched you fighting Santa last night," said Angus. He frowned. "I might have been thought of as a hero, too, if I'd fought Krampus out here in the street, where everyone could see."

"And if you were the person who'd beaten him," came an Austrian accent from behind them.

Angus turned to face the voice, approaching the thin man who crunched through the snow. "Christoph!" he said. He took the man in his arms, a big hand pummelling his back.

"Ow!" winced Christoph, pulling away from the hug.

"I'm sorry!" said Angus. "I thought Millie and Judith had healed you! I thought the wounds on your back had gone!"

Christoph smiled. "They have," he said. "But I don't think you're aware of your own strength. I've heard of bear hugs, but I've never received a wolf hug."

Angus broke into a wide grin, his eyes sparkling. "I'm glad you came!"

"Of course I came," said Christoph. "The invite mentioned stollen."

"Beer?" asked Angus.

"Beer," nodded Christoph.

As the two men made their way towards the pub, Christoph looked at the taller man. "You know it was me who killed Krampus, don't you? If either of us is a hero, it's me."

"Och," said Angus, placing an arm around his new friend's shoulder. "We're both heroes, Christoph."

As the unlikely pair headed for the pub, Millie became aware of a small crowd approaching her. With smiles on their faces, they stood in a little group, their winter attire giving them the appearance of carol singers.

She blushed as a round of applause rippled through the group, and a man raised his voice. "Thank you, Millie! Thanks to all of you who helped us last night! You'll never be forgotten in Kilgrettin!"

"Next, they'll be telling us that their ancestors will sing songs about us," whispered Judith, stifling a giggle.

Another round of applause went up, and Millie smiled. "Thank you," she said. "But please, it was our pleasure to help you last night."

A small man stepped forward. "Then eat with us," he said. "This feast is to celebrate Christmas and to thank you all for what you did. Please, enjoy our hospitality, and, as you can see, it's people who share the same qualities as you, who've made today so special."

As the crowd began drifting away, Millie walked with Judith and Maggie towards the Christmas tree. She lifted her head to the sky. "Reuben's taking his time," she said, a brief surge of nausea blooming as she recalled her worry for him the day before.

"He was busy eating fudge," said Judith. "He'll be

here when he gets a whiff of this feast." She stopped walking and gave a laugh. "Look at it!"

"It's really something, isn't it?" said Millie. "Paranormal and non-paranormal people having fun together, with no secrets between them anymore."

Millie stood still and took a moment to take in the events unfolding around her. With so much going on, her eyes darted across the town square, finding something new to focus on everywhere she looked.

First, she took in the table. As long as the tables she'd seen in photographs of the street parties that took place in Britain to mark the Queen's Silver Jubilee, it stretched through the square, laden with food.

Towering over it stood the Christmas tree, its already beautiful decorations embellished with pretty globes of magical lights which spun slowly, dancing with colour.

She smiled as she watched a young girl point a mittened hand at the tree, releasing a trickling stream of pink sparks which twisted through a tree branch, transforming into sparkling tinsel.

The four girls standing next to her watched in astonishment, bursting into cheers as the little girl cast another spell. As her friends cheered again, the young girl's cheeks glowed a proud rosy red, and she hugged the girl standing next to her.

"I never knew she and her mother were witches," said Maggie, her gaze following Millie's. "But look, it's wonderful, isn't it? The other kids are so accepting."

"It is wonderful," said Millie, her gaze finding a group of boys who stood in a semi-circle around a red-haired boy, who glanced at the others nervously.

At first, she thought the other boys were bullying him as they shouted at him, but then it became apparent they were urging him to do something.

The boy with red hair smiled, and then, with a theatrical snarl which reverberated through the square, his eyes blackened, and he opened his mouth, revealing gleaming fangs.

Taking a crouching position, he snarled again and then thrust himself upwards in a leap so high it made the other boys gasp.

Slamming a fist into the snow as he made an overly showy landing, the boy stood up and took a bow as his friends cheered and clapped. As the young vampire began laughing, his eyes were human again, and his fangs gone.

Crowding around him, his friends stared into his mouth, one of them prodding his gums with a finger.

Then, Millie watched Annie and the two witches who helped her. It seemed they were responsible for the feast, and they'd pulled out all the stops to create a Christmas spread that wouldn't have looked out of place on The Ghost of Christmas Present's table.

People lined both sides of the long table, laughing and drinking as they enjoyed each other's company.

Striding alongside the table, the three witches added the finishing touches to what was already a feat of spectacular magic.

With a flourish of her hand, one of the witches — a young lady with high cheekbones and a pretty smile, added another orb to the row already magically suspended above the table, moving gently on the breeze, the candles inside them casting a warm glow over the diners.

Another witch, an older woman wearing a colourful apron, aimed her hand at one of the only empty silver platters on the table. "Mashed potatoes and swede with grass-fed butter," she announced, as a hot dish of fluffy golden food appeared.

"I'm not sure why I never suspected she was a witch," said Maggie, smiling. "Helen runs a little café, and the food she serves is out of this world. Now I know why!"

With bacon and pancakes still heavy in her stomach, Millie's mouth watered anyway as she ran her eyes along the long line of food. Huge hams sat alongside dishes crammed with roast potatoes so golden they glowed.

Roast parsnips and carrots accompanied them, and vivid green vegetables shimmered beneath generous coatings of butter.

Pigs-in-blankets shared plates with stuffing, and giant jugs were filled to the brim with thick, velvety gravy, clouds of steam curling from them.

Millie sniffed the air, her stomach growling in protest as she caught the aroma of the thick bread sauce a man ladled onto his plate, finding space alongside the brussels sprouts dotted with pieces of crispy bacon.

Spaced evenly among the food, each on a large platter, were several large turkeys. Golden brown and surrounded by more roast potatoes, Millie could tell just by looking at them that they were melt-in-the-mouth moist.

As cutlery clinked on plates and wine glasses were raised in toasts, Millie eyed up the desserts, promising herself a piece of the rich Christmas pudding, adorned with a sprig of holly. Then she saw the gingerbread men and the butter cookies and made the decision that her New Year's resolution would be to lose the pounds she was about to gain.

As children's laughter arrived on the wind and more people took their seats at the table, a plump man seated near one of the turkeys got to his feet. Dressed in a Christmas sweater, he smiled at Millie and clinked his wine glass with a knife. "Merry Christmas, Millie," he said, as a hush drew over the table.

Millie smiled back, remembering how confused the poor man had been the night before. "Merry Christmas, Clive," she said.

His voice carrying through the snow-blanketed streets, Clive lifted his wine glass and raised a toast. "To Millie, and her family and friends," he boomed. He raised his glass higher as Christoph and Angus approached the table, their noses whiskey red. "To *everybody* who saved our town last night. Each and every one of you is now an integral part of this town, whether you've lived here all of your life or not."

"Hear, hear," said a lady seated near Clive.

Clive nodded at Christoph. "You've lived here for twenty years and haven't been accepted as part of the community because you made one mistake a long time ago. I'm sorry, and it would be an honour to be accepted as your friend."

A cheer lifted from the people seated at the table, and Christoph lifted the whiskey glass in his hand. "Thank you," he said. "It means a lot to me."

Then, Clive turned his attention to Millie, Judith and their father. "And, of course, a little close-knit family who arrived by flying car, just a few days ago. You'll forever be a part of this community. We'll never forget you. And the whole town hopes you'll visit often."

More cheers rose from the table, and Judith nudged Millie. "He's wrong, isn't he? Most of them are going to forget us completely when Henry has cast his spell."

"Unfortunately," replied Millie. "But not Clive. He's married to a witch. Henry will spare his memories."

As if having heard her, Clive extended an arm towards his wife and raised his glass again. "One more toast, ladies and gentlemen. To my wonderful wife, and to Helen and Racheal. They've delivered a wonderful feast!"

Rounds of applause rippled along the table, and

then Clive's expression changed. He took a sip of his wine and put his glass down alongside his plate. "There is one more thing that must be said," he began. "Some of us have been keeping secrets from the rest of you for a long time. I've been keeping the secret of who my wife really is, and she's hidden her true self from you all. There are a few people like my wife in Kilgrettin… some witches, and others werewolves or vampires. There are probably some who are still too timid to come forward, but I know we will respect their secrecy until the time they feel they can. None of us wanted to keep secrets from you, but I'm sure you can all understand why we did. The existence of paranormal people must remain a secret, for their sakes."

Rising quickly from her seat, a young woman got to her feet. "We're proud that we have such a wonderful community of paranormal people here in Kilgrettin, and I'm sure I speak for everybody when I say that your secret will remain here in this valley, never to leave. But if a rogue wind were to scatter the secret beyond the mountains, we would turn on that traitor and deny the existence of our secret community. We would keep you safe. You have our word!"

Chairs ploughed through snow as they were pushed backwards, and people jumped to their feet, clapping and cheering, their voices startling an eagle that flew overhead.

Then, as the cheers faded and people sat down, Millie spotted two more birds, one far smaller than the other, but both approaching the town centre. "It's Reuben," she said, pointing. "And Robin."

"I told you he'd be here when he smelled the food," said Judith.

As the birds approached, Clive extended an arm towards several empty seats at the centre of the table. "Please," he said. "Take a seat, all of you."

As Millie introduced Henry to Clive, the butcher's face lit up as Edna approached the table, a little girl by her side. The girl giggled as she produced sparks at her fingertips, which took on the form of a fairy which danced on her hand. The girl looked up at Edna. "Thank you," she said. "I'll practice every day."

"Edna!" said Clive, grinning broadly. He turned to his wife. "Look, Annie, Edna's here!"

As Edna became reacquainted with old friends, Henry took a seat alongside Millie, tucking a serviette into his shirt and appraising the plates of food with a hungry eye, his gaze hovering on the plate heaped with thick slabs of carrot cake and golden mince pies. "What does Edna think she's doing?" he said. "She should not have taught that young witch new tricks. When my spell has been cast, and human minds are scrubbed of the events that occurred here, the young girl will be forbidden from using magic, unless it's absolutely necessary. Creating dancing, mythological creatures is not absolutely necessary. It's a silly party trick."

Ignoring Henry, Millie offered her sister the other

end of a Christmas cracker, which tingled as her fingers curled around it. Judith grinned as she took her end and pulled.

Both girls laughed as the cracker tore in two, a puff of purple smoke rising from it. Then, a tiny creature peered from Millie's portion of the cracker and stepped onto the table. The tiny mouse — partially transparent, and dressed in a bobble hat and scarf, put a small paw to its mouth and cleared its throat. "What does Santa suffer from if he gets stuck down a chimney?" it squeaked.

Laughing, Millie shook her head. "I don't know," she said.

The mouse stood on tiptoes and giggled. "Claustrophobia!" Then, it lifted its hat, bowed at the waist, and vanished in a puff of smoke.

"Did you like it?" asked Annie, her eyes sparkling as she smiled at Millie. "It's my take on a Christmas cracker! The jokes inside them are always naff, but I thought they'd be funnier being delivered by a mouse!"

"I loved it," said Millie. "It was brilliant."

Leaning across the table, Sergeant Spencer filled Millie's glass with wine. "I think you deserve that," he said. "It's been an odd few days."

"I couldn't agree more," said Millie, bringing the glass to her lips. As spicy fruit coated her tongue, she glanced to her right as feathers brushed her cheek and Reuben landed on her shoulder. "You made it then," she said.

"I ran out of fudge," replied the cockatiel. "Robin and I finished the lot."

"Where is Robin?" asked Millie. "I saw you two flying together."

"Check your other shoulder," replied Reuben.

Moving slowly, so as not to startle the bird, Millie smiled at the robin perched on her left shoulder, his head cocked enquiringly. "Hello, Robin," she cooed.

"He doesn't speak," snapped Reuben.

"I'm being nice," said Millie, sipping her wine.

Peering at Henry Pinkerton, Reuben squawked. "Could you get any more food on that plate, Henry?" he asked. "You certainly seem to be having a good time for a *bah-humbug* who was quite miserable when he arrived today!"

Wiping the corner of his mouth with his serviette, Henry peered over his glasses at the cockatiel. "I don't know if it's the mountain air," he said. "But you seem to have become quite cheeky, Reuben. I suggest that when you return to Spellbinder Bay, you consider bringing a better attitude with you."

"Maybe," said Reuben. "Maybe not." He hopped from Millie's shoulder and landed on the table. Then he drew his head back and hammered his beak against an empty glass. "Speech!" he squawked. "Can I have your attention, Scottish people? I'd like to say a few words."

"Can we have a bit of silence, folks!" shouted Clive, tapping his own glass with a knife.

"Thank you, Clive the butcher, AKA Santa," said

Reuben, fluttering to the Christmas tree and landing on a low branch. He peered at the people below him. "Hello, Scottish people! Don't be afraid. I realise that a talking bird may frighten some of you, but I'm perfectly harmless… unless you cross me."

"We saw far worse than you last night!" yelled a man. "Don't worry. Nobody's scared of you!"

"Oh, I see," said Reuben. "Then, I shall continue. I never thought I'd be breaking bread with a Scot, let alone a whole rowdy clan of them. Still, here I am, perched above a table heaving with delicacies, ready to participate in a bite to eat with people who reside to the north of Hadrian's Wall." He paused, his eyes scanning his audience. "And, funnily enough, what I want to speak to you folks about is connected to birds *and* the subject of food." He whistled, and Robin fluttered from Millie's shoulder, landing beside him, giving a shrill chirp.

"Does he talk, too?" shouted a boy.

"No!" snapped Reuben. "Of course not!" He shook his head slowly. "I shall ignore that interruption. What I have to ask of the people of Kilgrettin is simple. The little fellow next to me is Robin. He's my friend, and he and other birds like him have been struggling to find food in this harsh, frozen environment. I'd like to beg of you, that after I've left, you could find it in your hearts to ensure Robin and his friends can keep their bellies full until spring arrives."

"Of course!" said a woman.

"I'll put food out every day," said another.

"You say that now," said Reuben. "But what are you going to do when Henry Pinkerton has wiped your memories of all paranormal events. I'm paranormal — so you won't remember my oration! You'll forget that I asked you, and Robin will die! I'm going to have to insist that the paranormal folk among you relay my message to the humans when their memories have left them. If you'd be so kind."

The silence hanging over the table intensified, and Millie shuffled in her seat. "Reuben," she hissed.

"What did he say?" asked Clive, staring across the table at Henry. "You're going to wipe the minds of non-paranormal people?"

"Not you," said Henry, placing his knife and fork on his plate, and removing the serviette from his shirt. "You're married to a witch."

"You're going to wipe our minds?" shouted a man. "You can't do that! Why would you do that?"

Reaching into the pocket in which Millie had seen him place the spell, Henry stood up. "I'm afraid it's my job," he said, putting the bottle on the table. "The whole reason for my existence is to protect the paranormal community."

"From who?" asked Clive. "From the people seated alongside you, who've had their whole world turned upside down, yet have accepted the paranormal community having only learned of them last night? Is that who you're protecting them from?"

"It only takes one person to whisper a secret," said Henry, removing the cork from the little bottle.

"We're a close-knit community," said an elderly man. "We all have secrets about one another, especially people who've been around as long as I have. We won't whisper their secret, we'll keep it locked away in our hearts. In the heart of Kilgrettin itself."

Sighing, Henry tilted the bottle. "I'm sorry," he said, using his fingertip to draw orange liquid from the neck, allowing it to twist in the air like a snake, preparing to cast it. "And should anybody in the paranormal community make themselves known to the townsfolk after the spell is cast, there will be dire consequences for them."

Aware of somebody standing next to her, Millie turned to see the young vampire with red hair. He tugged at Henry's waistcoat. "Mister?" he said.

Peering down at him, Henry raised an eyebrow. "Yes?"

"Please don't wipe their memories," he said. "If you wipe their memories, all my friends will forget who I really am, and I'll have to go back to pretending I'm someone I'm not again. I want to be me. I want my friends to like me for who I really am."

Placing a hand on the boy's head, Henry ruffled his curls. "One day, you'll understand why I have to do it, young sir."

"What about me?" shouted Christoph. "I'm human, but I helped out yesterday! I killed a beast which would have hurt many people if I hadn't stopped it. Are you going to wipe my memory, and the new friendships I've created?"

Henry took a deep breath and lifted his hand, the spell following his fingers as it sparkled and fizzed. "You'll be able to enjoy the rest of the day, but after a night's sleep, your memories will be gone. I had intended to cast the spell a little less publicly, but Reuben forced my hand. I'm sorry."

"No!" said Annie. "Please don't!"

Looking away from the witch, Henry moved his hand across the table, the spell morphing into a bubble which quickly increased in size until it looked ready to burst. Then, he turned his eyes on Annie. "I'm sorry," he said, his other hand moving swiftly towards the bulging bubble. "It's for the best."

Chapter 26

As horrified faces watched Henry preparing to cast the spell, Millie experienced a rush of anger.

What he was doing was wrong.

The residents of Kilgrettin seated at the table, and those who'd decided to spend Christmas Day at home, had accepted the paranormal people they'd discovered had been living among them for so long.

The people of the isolated town had been friends for years, decades even — their families stretching back centuries, helping each other, living alongside one another.

The fact that a tiny minority of people in town had suddenly revealed themselves to be different, had done nothing to weaken the strong bonds that tied the population together. In fact, the bonds appeared tighter.

As Henry's hand sped towards the balloon of

magic, Millie saw the little vampire boy with red hair staring at her, his eyes communicating a terrible disappointment that no child should exhibit on Christmas Day.

With no conscious effort on her behalf, Millie realised she was standing, her seat toppling to the snow behind her. Then her hand was tingling. And then, as bright as the reflection of the winter sun on the Kilted Stag's windows, the spell exploded from her fingers.

At first, she wasn't sure what had happened, but then, as Henry's hand neared the bubble of magic, his fingertips millimetres away, he let out a gasp as Millie's spell created a wall of energy which protected the bubble.

Angry red sparks rose from Henry's hand as he withdrew it like a child testing a flame.

Having prevented Henry from activating the spell, Millie's magic proceeded to wrap itself around the bubble, applying pressure, making it vibrate violently.

Then, as if it were a party balloon pricked by a pin, it popped, the sound echoing across the valley — hanging in the air even as the spell vanished and Henry turned to Millie, his face angrier than she'd ever seen it.

"How dare you!" he said, the people at the table shifting uneasily in their seats. "You've overstepped the mark, Millie Thorn."

"It's not right," said Millie. "These people deserve

to live how they want to live, not how you want them to."

"I could punish you, Millie," said Henry. "You know what happens to members of our community who cross the line."

"You're not going to send Millie to The Chaos," said Edna, getting to her feet. "You love the girl. We all know that."

"And you'd have to get through me first," said Sergeant Spencer, standing up.

"And me," said Judith.

Rolling his shoulders and taking a deep breath, Henry sighed. He placed a fingertip over the little bottle, his eyes still on Millie as a strand of orange energy snaked from the neck. "I always make enough of any spell to allow myself a second chance, in case unforeseen circumstances present themselves."

As the strand of energy began twisting and quivering, morphing slowly into another bubble of magic, he stared at Millie over his glasses. "I trust there will be no unforeseen circumstances this time, or I may not be so forgiving."

As Henry's hand moved quickly towards the bubble, Millie's fingers throbbed with energy. As she prepared to prevent Henry once more, a voice rang out from behind her. "Henry! Stop!"

The voice momentarily distracting Henry, Millie took the opportunity to cast her spell, once more preventing him from wiping the memories of the Kilgrettin townsfolk. Red sparks erupted from his hand as his fingers brushed Millie's energy, and his face darkened as he withdrew his fingers.

Glaring at Millie, Henry opened his mouth to speak, but then looked towards the voice as startled cries began rising from the table. "Josephine," he said. "What is this?"

Looking towards the voice, too, Millie watched open-mouthed as the apparition of her mother drifted towards them across the snow.

It wasn't the vision of her mother that caught her breath, though. It was the silvery forms of hundreds of people who glided behind her, snowflakes harmlessly piercing their bodies as the army of ghosts moved as one through the town.

"What is this?" repeated Henry.

"These people are residents of Kilgrettin, too," said Josephine, smiling down at the ghostly young boy who walked alongside her, a flat cap on his head and a teddy bear in his hand. "They've wandered the shadows for too long. They deserve to see their families on Christmas Day."

Then, the wailing scream of a woman pierced the silence which hung like a cloud over the table. Casting her chair to the floor, the elderly woman struggled to her feet, allowing her walking stick to drop to the snow.

Sobbing, she hobbled towards the approaching figures, her wails becoming louder as she neared Josephine and the little boy.

Throwing herself to the snow, she knelt in front of

the child, her hands passing through him as she reached for his smiling face.

"Mummy!" said the boy, his arms travelling through the old woman as he attempted to hug her. "You look older, Mummy, but your eyes are the same. Kind, like I remember."

"Oh, Sammy!" said the old lady. "It's been so long. That's why, my sweet son. I'm old now."

"I'm sorry I left Mummy," said the boy. "I'm sorry I fell in the water. I was trying to show Teddy the fish, but I slipped. It didn't hurt. It was like going to sleep."

Oh, Sammy," sobbed the woman. "I've always prayed that you didn't suffer. I still pray. Every single day." Her eyes swollen with tears, the woman looked up at Josephine. "You did this?" she asked. "You brought my boy back?"

"These people have always been in the shadows," said Josephine. "But there wasn't enough magic in Kilgrettin to bring them forward. They knew they had to remain hidden, too — although now and again one or two have made themselves known."

"So I did see a ghost!" said a man's voice near Millie. "I knew it!"

"How long will my boy be here?" asked the old lady. She smiled at her son. "Although one fleeting moment would be enough for me, Sammy. I've waited for sixty years."

Josephine looked towards the table. "How long Sammy remains is down to Henry Pinkerton," she said. "All these people can become a part of your community if Henry decides not to wipe your memories. There's enough magic in the air now to bring them forward, and the witches of Kilgrettin can sustain the magic if Henry allows it."

As Josephine spoke, another woman ran towards the apparitions. Stumbling in the snow, she sprang quickly to her feet. "Dad! It's you!" she yelled, her words wracked with sobs. "Dad!"

Stepping from the shimmering rows of ghosts, a middle-aged man wearing a cardigan walked towards his daughter. "Hello, Emily," he said, opening his arms. "I've missed you."

Then, drinks spilled and chairs fell as more people leapt to their feet and hurried through the snow, shouting names and crying as they recognised loved ones.

"I can't allow this," murmured Henry, as scores of ghosts broke rank and glided towards the crowds of people approaching them, like two armies meeting on a winter battlefield.

Millie looked at him. "Why?" she said. "Do you remember what I went through to see my mother? To bring her back from the other side?"

"Of course I do," said Henry. "But this is not the same. This town is not protected by a concealment spell like Spellbinder Bay is. Spellbinder Bay is a paranormal town, and humans just happen to live there, oblivious of our existence."

"What *is* the same," said Millie, "is that Sammy's mother loves her son as dearly as I love my mother.

Would you prevent me from seeing my mother again, Henry? Knowing how much it would hurt me?"

Refusing to look at her, Henry shook his head. "It's not the same. I'm going to wipe these people's memories. They won't even remember seeing the ghosts of their loved ones."

"But that old lady will remember her grief," said Millie. "And she'll continue hoping every day that her son didn't suffer. You won't just be taking her memories of today from her — you'll be returning something too — the agony that just slid from her face when she found out that Sammy hadn't suffered."

Henry closed his eyes. He remained silent for a moment and then turned his head slowly and glared at Millie. "Very well," he said. "Be it on your head. I'll speak to you when you return to Spellbinder Bay. Be prepared."

Then, with a dark expression on his face that Millie had never seen him wear before, he vanished, the air where he'd been standing crackling with static electricity.

Looking at her father, who had remained standing, ready to defend his daughter had he been needed, Millie gave a flat smile. "I think I've just made an enemy of Henry Pinkerton," she said.

"Give him time," said Edna, wrapping an arm around her. "He's very fond of you, Millie, but you've forced him to go against his instincts. He's angry. For now."

Placing her head on the woman's shoulder, Millie smiled. "And you've just lost your ride home."

"I'll travel with you three," said Edna. "If there's room in that car of yours."

"The car won't be ready for another week," said Sergeant Spencer. "Even magic can't repair the damage done to a car when a herd of flying reindeers dragging a sleigh slams into it."

"Then I shall have some time to become reacquainted with some old friends in Kilgrettin," said Edna.

"What about your mother, Millie?" asked Judith. "She came with Henry, too."

"Don't worry about me," said Josephine, gliding to Millie's side. "There's plenty of magic in Kilgrettin now. I can travel whenever I like."

"Look what you did, Mum," said Millie, watching people greeting ghosts, laughter and tears flying through the air as easily as the snowballs that children had begun throwing. "You've brought families together."

As a man's angry voice joined the laughter, Sergeant Spencer pointed. "Enemies, too."

"Oh no," said Josephine, hiding a smile as a short, elderly man with a belly that bounced when he ran, scurried after the ghost of a taller man who laughed as he evaded the human.

The short man yelled again, pausing for breath as he passed right through the ghost he was pursuing, his breath billowing above him. "You bawbag!" he yelled.

"I knew I'd lent my lawnmower to you! You denied it for ten years, Jock! When I was helping Betty deal with your belongings, I was livid when I saw it sitting there in the corner of your shed, hidden under a sheet!"

"Go easy on him, Osie," said an old woman hobbling towards them, her eyes alive with joy. "Leave some for me! I want to find out whose perfume that was in the glovebox of his car!"

"Betty!" yelled the ghost, hurrying towards his wife. "I've missed you!"

"I've missed you, too, you big lummox," said Betty, staring up into his eyes.

Placing a ghostly hand on the little woman's face, Jock smiled. "I can explain about the perfume," he said. "It was —"

Shaking her head, Betty placed a finger on the ghost's lips. She pulled her hand from inside his head, and tried again, this time, her finger brushing his mouth. "It doesn't matter, Jock. It was five years ago. I don't care. I'll have plenty of time to find out when I join you forever." She stood on tiptoes and placed her lips next to his. "I love you, Jock. I never told you that enough before you went."

"I love you, too, Betty," replied Jock. "Merry Christmas."

Wiping a tear from her eye, Millie gazed around at her family, then she stared up at the Christmas tree. She smiled as she watched Robin and Reuben snatching scraps of food from the air, as children stood below the tree, throwing them skyward.

His eye catching Millie's, Reuben squawked. "It's the most wonderful time of the year!"

Millie nodded. "It is," she said.

"Then let's enjoy it," said her mother. "None of you have eaten yet. Let's sit down and have Christmas dinner together. It's your first Christmas dinner with your father and sister, Millie. I might not be able to eat, but I'll cherish the memory of seeing you celebrating together."

"You too, Edna," said Sergeant Spencer, sitting down.

As Edna lowered herself into the chair next to Millie, she reached for her hand. "I've been a witch for a long time," she said, her voice low. "I can sense you're worried about Henry. Please don't. I'm sure everything will be okay."

Millie nodded. She hoped Edna was correct because the thought of being on the wrong side of Henry Pinkerton sent little shivers of cold along her spine.

Then, as her father and sister pulled a cracker together, ejecting a tiny giggling mouse, Millie saw it. A flash of colour further along the table. In an instant, she knew what she was looking at.

As the colours briefly became the bright patterns on a smart waistcoat, a pair of hands appeared in mid-air, grasping the plate laden with carrot cake and mince pies.

Then, just before the plate, the hands and the waistcoat vanished again, Henry's face flashed into existence.

He looked her way, and his lips formed the beginnings of a smile. Behind the glasses which reflected the joyous scene, Millie saw an eyelid close, and then open. *A wink.*

Reaching for a dish brimming with roast potatoes, Millie turned to Edna. "I'm sure everything will be okay, too."

The End

Also by Sam Short

The Spellbinder Bay Series

Book One — Witch Way to Spellbinder Bay

Book Two — Broomsticks And Bones

Book Three — Spells And Cells

Book Four — Snowmen and Sorcery

Don't forget to read the complete Water Witch Cozy Paranormal Series!

The first series by Sam Short.

Book one — Under Lock and Key

Book Two — Four and Twenty Blackbirds

Book Three — An Eye For an Eye

Book Four — A Meeting of Minds

Try this one, too!

A Dash of Pepper by Sam Short

About the Author

Sam Short loves witches, goats, and narrowboats. He really enjoys writing fiction that makes him laugh — in the hope it will make others laugh too!
You can find him at the places listed below — he'd love to see you there!

www.samshortauthor.com
email — sam@samshortauthor.com

Made in the USA
Middletown, DE
06 January 2021

30911845R00161